About the Author

Paula worked as a bank manager for over twenty years before retiring. She lives in Somerset with her husband and has two grown-up sons and four granddaughters. Since retiring she fills her days with writing, going to the gym and anything family related.

Maisie - The Early Years

Paula Wilkes

Maisie - The Early Years

Olympia Publishers

London

www.olympiapublishers.com

OLYMPIA PAPERBACK EDITION

A CIP catalogue record for this title is
available from the British Library.

ISBN: 978-1-78830-033-9

This is a work of fiction.
Names, characters, places and incidents originate from the writer's
imagination. Any resemblance to actual persons, living or dead, is purely
coincidental.

First Published in 2017

Olympia Publishers
60 Cannon Street
London
EC4N 6NP

Printed in Great Britain

Dedication

This book is dedicated to my wonderful mother, Daphne James.

Pay Day

As Maisie's mammy hurried down the old wooden stairs of their one up one down cottage, her arms filled with blankets and pillows from the children's beds, she looked at Maisie and whispered, 'It's pay day.' Maisie knew that this meant that her lovely, decent dada would be turned into a foul drunken wife beater. She watched as her mother pulled the heavy wooden cabinet away from the wall to reveal a hidden cubby hole beneath the stairs. She hurriedly made up a makeshift bed and as each of Maisie's three little sisters filed past her she handed them a hunk of bread told them to stay nice and quiet. 'Now, no matter what,' she said to Maisie. 'As the oldest, you keep these little ones quiet.' She noticed the worried look on Maisie's face. 'It's all right, pigeon, I'll see you in the morning. But please be quiet.'

With that, Maisie entered the small cubby hole and cuddled down with her sisters. How she wished that her mammy would crawl in and hide as well, but when she had asked Mammy to do this in the past she had told her, "That will make him even more angry and then you kids will get a beating."

It was very late when Maisie heard the door crash open. She could tell from the way that her father was talking that he had stopped at The Anvil for what the men called, "a swift one". It seemed a bit of a ritual with the men from the pit who all seemed to need to drink their wages away without thought or care for how their families would be fed for the next two weeks. Maisie heard some coins been thrown onto the table.

'Is that it?' came her mammy's voice. 'How do I pay rent and feed the little ones on that?'

The sound of a chair grating on the flagstone floor made Maisie shudder. 'Don't you come the high and mighty with me, a man can't even have a drink to wash the soot out his lungs,' was the angry reply. This was followed by something hitting the floor and her mammy's pitiful moans. Maisie didn't want to hear any more and buried her head deep in her pillow, pulling the sides up to block out the sounds of her mammy's beating.

Maisie woke with a start, what was all the noise? It sounded as if their small house had been invaded. The upstairs floor creaked and groaned under what sounded like a hundred boots.

'Madam, I'm telling you there are no children here,' came a very stern voice.

'If they're not here, where are they?'

Maisie suddenly realised that it was their nana's voice. 'Nana, Nana,' she shouted and bracing her back against the heavy wooden cabinet, she tried to push it out of the way.

'Hold up, young lady,' came another male voice and with this the cabinet started to move.

'Blimey, Sarge, I've never seen anything like it.'

With this the three younger girls started to cry, Maisie turned to see not one but three policemen peering in at them.

'Get out of my way.' Nana's voice made the policemen jump 'Well, well, so this is where she kept you safe, is it?'

'Nana, we've done nothing wrong,' Maisie started to cry.

'Don't be silly, child, they're not here for you.' The old woman gestured at the policemen.

One by one the little sisters emerged into the bright light of the downstairs room. They could hear their nana talking to the oldest of the three policemen. 'Well I'll have to take them for now, there is no-one else, but how I shall feed them I don't know.' With this, the two shook their heads in that knowing adult way.

Mrs Callow, Maisie's nana, glanced over her shoulder at the terrified youngsters. 'Right, you lot, come on.' With this she turned on her heel and marched out of the door.

'Where we going, Nana?' Charlotte, the youngest sister asked, but Mrs Callow just kept walking, her head held high, as the little troop made their way down the street. Maisie noticed that the women gossiping on their doorsteps suddenly fell quiet as they passed.

'Poor little things, everyone knew he would do for her one day,' a woman muttered as they passed.

After another ten minutes they arrived at Nana's house. On entering, Maisie was surprised to see that her Grandad was already at home. None of the men Maisie knew were ever at home in the morning, unless it was Sunday.

'Well, he finally did it.' Mrs Callow's voice stammered as if she was about to cry.

'Where is he?' demanded her husband. Maisie had never heard her Grandad angry and this made her shudder. He was a big man, at least six feet tall and although now in his fifties, still had the physique of a younger man. Mammy had always said it was the work that he did that kept him fit, no new-fangled gyms for him, not that they would have been able to afford it.

'Huh, he's gone. He scarpered before the police got there.' Mrs Callow slumped down in the chair. 'How are we going to manage?'

With this, Maisie's grandad got up from the chair and ushered the children towards the stairs. 'Go and make up the beds. Maisie, help the little ones.'

The three sisters ran up the stairs. Half way up Maisie stopped. 'Grandad, where is Mammy? We haven't seen her today.'

He shook his head slowly and she would have sworn that he wiped away a tear. 'Just be a good girl and do as I say.' With this, he walked back across the room and sat down next to Nana.

Three months later

The four little sisters rounded the corner into Liverpool Street, they'd been living here for the last three months. Maisie had found it particularly hard. As the oldest she was expected to help Nana with the household chores; she had come to hate Mondays as this was wash day. It was her job to turn the old mangle's handle whilst Nana fed the clothes through. By the end of the day every muscle in her body seemed to be screaming with pain and she would barely have enough energy to climb the steep stairs up to the loft where she and her little sisters slept.

'Hurry up, you girls,' shouted her nana, who unusually was waiting for them on the doorstep. 'Come on, come on.' The three little ones ran full pelt down the street towards the house. Maisie tried to hurry up but the heavy shopping basket slowed her down. 'Maisie, for goodness' sake get a move on,' came the woman's angry cry.

'I'm sorry, Nana,' was her pitiful response as she tried to quicken her step. As soon as she reached the door, Mrs Callow snatched the basket from her.

'All of you go up and wash your faces, brush your hair and put on your clean dresses,' she barked. 'Oh, and don't come down until I call you.' She had just finished issuing her orders when the old wooden front door shuddered under a thunderous knock. 'Oh no, oh no, they're early.' Mrs Callows hands flew up to her, hair quickly tidying the bun at the back of her head. 'Go on, you lot and remember, don't come down until I call you.'

The four girls stood in front of Nana's visitor, who was looking them up and down intently. 'These three I can take,' she pointed to the three little ones, 'but this one is too old.' She nodded her head towards Maisie.

'Oh well, three out of four is better than nothing,' replied Mrs Callow. With this she turned towards Maisie. 'Go upstairs and pack the little ones' belongings.' Maisie opened her mouth to speak but was quickly silenced by the look on her nana's face; she obediently did as she was told.

'Now, girls,' she heard the lady saying to her little sisters, 'You are going on an adventure. Have any of you ever ridden in a pony and trap?' The three little ones shook their heads.

Maisie suddenly felt very afraid. 'Please don't take them away from me,' she pleaded as she lumbered down the stairs under the weight of her sisters' belongings.

'Be quiet, girl,' snapped her nana, snatching the items from Maisie's trembling hands. With that the sisters were ushered out of the door. As they climbed the little ladder attached to the pony cart Martha, the oldest of the three, shouted over her shoulder, 'We're going on an adventure, see you later, Maisie.'

All Maisie could do was to watch the three most precious people in the world disappear out of sight. As the pony and trap rounded the corner at the end of the street, she stood in the road and listened as hard as she could, trying to hear the clip clop of the ponys hooves. 'Nana, please don't do this, they are all that I have,' she wailed. 'Please, Nana, please.'

Without a backward glance the older woman stepped back into the house and slammed the door shut.

One Year later

As usual on a Tuesday morning Maisie was on her hands and knees, scrubbing the old tiled floor in her nanas house. Her hands hurt from the calluses that covered them, from the work that Nana gave her to do. She had only stopped for a minute to rub her aching shoulders when her nana's stern voice made her jump. 'I have never known such a lazy girl as you.' With this she felt a sharp kick to her bottom. 'Well, my girl, you'll soon realise how lucky you were living here. Get yourself washed and put on your Sunday dress, and be sharp about it.'

She was about to ask why, when she caught a glimpse of her nana's face. She didn't bother to wait but ran up the stairs to the loft.

Ten minutes later she was standing in front of the older woman.

'Good lord, girl, look at your hair.' With this the older woman snatched up an old comb and started to yank it through Maisie's long dark hair. 'How many times have I told you that your hair must be up, not left loose like a little child?' The woman twisted and pulled her hair until she was satisfied that it looked at least half decent. 'Pick up that sack, you've made us late.' With this Mrs Callow hurried out of the house.

'Late? Late for what?' Maisie asked as she ran to keep up.

'Never you mind, you'll find out soon enough,' was the short-tempered reply.

The pair hurried down street after street. Maisie had never been this far from home. Suddenly the old lady turned into a little alley which was half hidden by an old broken gate. The alley smelled badly and Maisie had to stop herself from gagging. As suddenly as they had entered the alley they emerged into a cobbled courtyard; in the middle of the yard stood the biggest horse Maisie had ever seen. It was harnessed to a blue and gold wagon that was full of barrels and what looked like sacks of meat. Two men were standing at the far end and on seeing them emerge from the alley, the smaller of the two shouted, 'About bloody time, I was just about to leave.'

Both men started to walk back across the yard towards the horse and wagon. 'So, this is Maisie, the smaller man stated. 'My name's Jack, now quickly hop up or we'll be late, then there really will be trouble.'

Maisie looked from the man to her nana. 'Why do I need to hop up?' she whispered to no-one in particular.

'No time for explanations now, do as you're told.' Maisie put one foot on the little step of the wagon and without any further notice the older woman gave her a mighty shove and, Maisie found herself on the seat at the front of the wagon. Jack switched the reins and made a clicking noise with his tongue. At this the huge horse started to move forward.

Nana gave a shout. 'Hey, I think you've forgotten something.' With this, Jack took a little bag from his waistcoat pocket and threw it to the woman. As she caught it Maisie heard a clink of coins and the realisation of her situation suddenly hit her. Nana had sold her, just like she had sold her sisters a year ago.

Jack looked at the young girl. He could tell that she was frightened and he wondered why on earth a grandmother would sell her own flesh and blood. 'How old are you?' He spoke gently to the young girl.

'I think I'm ten,' she mumbled. Tears started to run down her cheeks and she clutched the sack bag to her. 'What is going to happen to me, sir?'

Jack tugged on the reins and the horse immediately stopped. 'What, are you telling me that no-one has told you where you are going?' He shook his head in disbelief. On getting no reply, he continued, 'Maisie, you are coming to live at Wilton Park.' One look at her face told him that she had no idea what he was talking about. 'Wilton Park is owned by Lord Willaby, and your nana has agreed that you will come and work as a helper to cook. From what I can see, you'll be far better off at the Park than living with your nana. Just make sure that you do everything that Cook asks you to do, no back chat and you'll be fine.' He gave Maisie a kind smile. 'Have you eaten today?' Maisie shook her head and he handed her a little parcel. 'Go on, girl, fill your boots. Cooks best cake, that is.' Maisie couldn't believe her eyes. She had never been given a whole slice of cake and she greedily tucked into it.

Wilton Park

'Welcome to your new home, Maisie.' Jack swung the cart to the right. 'This is Wilton Park'

Maisie couldn't believe her eyes. It appeared to her that the drive went on for miles and at the end, even at this distance, was the biggest house Maisie had ever seen. To the left side of the drive lay parkland which gently sloped down to a large lake; flowering bushes and huge trees had been planted to draw the eye towards the lake. The lawn to the left disappeared into a wooded area. To the right of the drive cattle grazed and Maisie could see in the distance men working in the fields; their voices could just be made out and Maisie caught a faint sound of laughter. This made her smile. Maybe this wouldn't be such a bad place to live.

Jack clicked his tongue and the horse started to trot. 'Best hurry or Cook will be cross with me.' He caught the frightened look that crossed Maisie's face. 'It's all right, girl, I'm joking.' He smiled at her and she gave him such a sweet smile that, again he couldn't understand how her grandmother could be so cold to send her away.

As they drew nearer to the mansion, Maisie gasped, 'Oh my, how will I clean all of this?' She thought about how hard it had been to keep Nana's house clean and keep up with the laundry, but this place was a thousand times bigger.

Jack started to laugh so hard that Maisie was afraid that he would fall off the cart. 'Oh, Maisie, you won't be cleaning this place on your own. Lord Willaby has lots of staff, butler, cook and housemaids, not counting the gardener's, grooms and farm workers. So don't you go fretting. Like I said before, you do exactly what Cook tells you to do and no back chat and you will be just fine.' With this, he nudged Maisie's arm with his elbow and winked at her.

The horse suddenly turned to the right, following a small roadway that led around the side of the mansion, down a small hill and into an enclosed yard. All the way around the yard were various open-fronted buildings. Some had logs piled up in neat stacks; others had various sized barrels stored in them. Through an opening in the wall, Maisie glimpsed a young girl picking apples off one of the many trees growing there.

Jack brought the cart to a halt in front of a large wooden door. 'Right, let's get you inside.' With this he jumped down and ran around to help Maisie down.

'Jack, will I really be all right?' Maisie's lip trembled as she fought to hold back the tears. Jack gently put his arm around her shoulders and steered her through the big wooden door.

'About time—' Cook started to turn towards the door, but her voice trailed off as she noticed the little girl shaking next to Jack.

'This is Maisie.' Jack spoke gently. He remained standing next to Maisie with his arm still around her shoulders. 'Can you spare me a moment, Cook, for a private chat? Maisie, why don't you go and sit next to the fire on that little stool?' He pushed her gently towards the fire.

With that Jack and Cook walked to the other end of the kitchen and started to whisper. Every now and again Maisie would catch a phrase or word. 'What? Oh, that woman,' came Cooks voice. 'Jack, are you serious?'

After what seemed like hours, Jack walked back towards Maisie. 'Remember what I told you.' He ruffled Maisie's hair and walked out of the door.

'Right then,' Cook spoke as she bustled around the kitchen. 'We had better get you sorted. Did Jack leave your belongings outside?' Maisie, who was still clutching the hessian sack, looked down at it. 'Oh no, is that everything?' Cook tutted. 'What on earth was that woman thinking?' she said, more to herself than to Maisie. 'Good job that you will be in uniform. We must get something done to that hair.' Maisie put her hand up to her hair, which had now started falling out of the grips that her nana had forced in, was it really only this morning? So much had happened since then.

The big wooden door swung open and a girl came stumbling into the kitchen, a large basket of apples in her arms. 'Blimey, Cook, that was hard work,' she puffed. Whilst straightening up she noticed the little girl sitting next to the fire. 'Oh, hello, you must be Maisie, I'm Mary Black.' She eyed Maisie, taking in the old clothes and untidy hair. 'Shall I show her where she will be sleeping?' She directed this at Cook.

'Try and get her smartened up, I can't take her to meet Mrs Dean looking like that.' Cook rubbed her hand across her forehead. 'I hope we have a uniform that small.' Cook pointed at Maisie.

'Come on.' Mary started towards a small door at the side of the big black cooking range. Maisie quickly got to her feet and ran after her. 'You didn't bring much with you.' Mary eyed the hessian sack in the smaller girls hand.

'It's everything I have,' Maisie said defensively.

'Sorry, didn't mean to offend,' was Mary's reply as she pulled at a cupboard door. Inside, stacked neatly, were different articles of clothing. After holding several garments up against Maisie she nodded. 'This is the best we can do for now. Come on.'

They both climbed the narrow stone stairs up one floor and then another and another until they finally reached the top of the house. 'Now, you never, ever go through that door.' Mary pointed at a door at the end of the corridor. 'That's the male servants' quarters. If you're found in there,' she made a cutting motion across her throat, 'you will be out on your ear, do you understand?' Maisie nodded. 'It doesn't matter who tells you to go through there, don't do it.'

They walked to the opposite end of the corridor. 'This is our room.' Mary opened the door and ushered Maisie in. The room had a sloping roof with a little window, just like Maisie's room at her nana's. There was a picture of Jesus on the wall and, underneath this stood a small table with a wash basin and jug on it. There was a small cupboard to the left of this and opposite were two single iron frame beds.

'This is my bed.' Mary flopped down on the bed. Maisie walked over and sat on the other. To her surprise it felt quite comfortable; the one she had slept on at her nana's had been so hard that it felt as if she was sleeping on the floor.

'Right, come on, there's water in the jug. Give yourself a wash and we will see what we can do to that hair.' Mary started searching through the cupboard as Maisie washed herself. The water was very cold, but she was used to washing in cold water, in fact that was all she had ever washed in. "No hot water for you", her nana had always said. Even when the four little girls had lived with her, the smaller three had been allowed tepid water in the tin bath that would be brought in and placed in front of the fire. Maisie always had to wash after them in the same water.

'I knew I had some,' came the joyful screech from inside the cupboard. She emerged with a narrow piece of ribbon in her hand. 'Come here and let me do your hair.'

The two girls walked back into the kitchen. Cook was still bustling about the kitchen but now there was another girl working at one of the long tables. Both stopped what they were doing as the door opened.

'Goodness,' exclaimed Cook. 'Well, don't you look just fine. Well done, Mary.' The older girl beamed at the praise.

'This can't be the little urchin that you were talking about,' the other girl laughed. 'You look just fine. I'm Jennie O'Keefe. From your uniform I guess you are going to be working as a scullery maid with Mary.' Both girls were dressed in grey self-striped dresses with plain grey collars and white aprons.

Maisie looked at Mary, who nodded enthusiastically. 'Be nice to have someone to help me,' she beamed.

'Um, Cook.' Mary gave a little cough. 'I think that Maisie is hungry, she arrived after we had eaten.' She looked down at her boots.

'Oh, my goodness, I didn't think. Jennie, can you give her some of that cold pie and a slice of bread.' Cook pointed to a table in the corner of the kitchen. 'Sit there, and Jennie, you had better give Mary the same as a reward for her hard work.'

Mary clapped her hands and pulled Maisie to the table. Both girls tucked into the cold pie and bread as if they had never eaten before, although for Maisie, she had never tasted anything so nice and wiped her plate clean with her bread. 'Thank you, Cook,' she said in a timid voice. 'That was lovely.' Cook looked surprised for a moment but as she turned away, Maisie was sure that she was smiling.

Settling In

Maisie followed Cook along the stone corridor. After a while Cook stopped and knocked on a door. A faint voice could be heard calling, 'Come in.'

Cook gave Maisie a quick look, making sure that she was presentable. 'Now listen. You only speak when you're spoken to, do you understand?' Maisie nodded.

'Good afternoon, Mrs Dean, I hope that we are not interrupting anything. But as discussed earlier, our new scullery maid has arrived.' Cook looked at Maisie and gave her a little push forward.

'As I see.' With this Mrs Dean, who had been seated at a big oak desk in front of the window, stood up. She was a tall, slender woman with her blond hair pulled back in a very tight bun at the nape of her neck. She was dressed in a black dress that had a pure white lace collar, and at her waist, hanging from her belt was a bunch of keys that jangled when she moved. 'My goodness, she is very small, are you sure that she is up to the job?' This was directed at Cook, at which Cook just nodded but didn't speak.

'Well, young lady, as you have just heard I am Mrs Dean. All of the female staff answer to me, do you understand?' With this Maisie followed Cooks lead and nodded without speaking.

'Cook, has anyone explained the house rules and etiquette?' Without waiting for Cook to respond she continued, 'if not, then this must be a priority and I expect you to ask one of the more senior girls to sit with her and explain everything to her today.' With this she turned and returned to her seat. Cook gave Maisies arm a tug and they both left the room.

Once outside in the corridor Cook clicked her tongue. 'Well how does she expect me to spare one of my best girls at this time of day, with afternoon tea and then the suppers to get ready?' she muttered to herself as they both marched back down the corridor. On re-entering the kitchen Maisie was surprised to see another two girls in the kitchen. Jennie was standing at the long table near the window and was busily kneading dough, which she was making into little balls and placing them on a baking tray. One of the girls was chopping vegetables, whilst the other was stirring a large pot of something, which smelt delicious on the large cooking range. As they entered the kitchen all three girls stopped what they were doing, but one look at Cook's face made the two younger girls hurriedly return to their work; only Jennie remained looking at Cook.

'What does she think we do in here all day?' Cook blasted. 'Get one of my senior girls to sit and explain the house rules and etiquette,' Cook mimicked Mrs Dean's voice. 'We have all the time in the world, don't we?' she announced to no-one in particular.

'Peggy,' Jennie directed this to the girl chopping vegetables. 'Please make Cook a nice cup of tea.' With this, Peggy moved quickly to put the kettle on. She was very small in stature but Maisie noticed that she was nearly as wide as she was tall.

'Hello, you must be Maisie, I heard that you were joining the merry team.' With this, Peggy gave a hearty laugh and the other new girl, who Maisie found out later was called Nancy, joined in.

'Now, you two, stop that and get on with your work. Peggy, where's that cup of tea?' Jennie said this whilst sitting Cook at the table in the corner of the kitchen. 'Sit there for a minute and enjoy your tea, we can manage for a few minutes and don't go worrying about house rules and the like. I can sort that out.' With that Jennie gave the two girls a stern look, at which they quickly returned to their duties.

'Maisie, come and sit here and I will explain the basics to you whilst I work.' Maisie did as she was told. Jennie drew in a long breath and started explaining to Maisie, 'Unless someone speaks to you directly you are to remain silent.

'You will rise at 6.00 a.m. and be in the kitchen by 6.30 a.m. washed, dressed and with your hair tied up and out of sight under your cap.

'Along with Mary, you will ensure that the kitchen fire and range are fully lit and that the kettle is on so that when Cook and I arrive a cup of tea is ready for us.

'After this you will lay the table in the servants' hall for breakfast.

'By this time Peggy will be making a start on the servants' breakfasts and you will assist her.

'I will be getting trays ready for the family, along with Nancy. You are NOT to touch these trays.

'After the servants have had their breakfast you will wash the dishes and ensure that the kitchen surfaces and floor are clean, after which you will scrub the kitchen passages, the pantries and the scullery.

'The table in the servants' hall will need to be re-laid for their morning tea, after which you will wash the dishes and ensure that the servants' hall is clean ready for dinner. If Cook or I need any extra help you will assist by cleaning vegetables for the family's luncheon.

'At all times, it is your duty to ensure that the kitchen is kept spotless and that everything is washed up and stored away immediately.

'You will lay the table in the servants' hall for their afternoon tea and again clear and wash up everything.

'You will assist Nancy with preparing vegetables for the family's dinner and the servants' supper, again ensuring that the kitchen is kept spotless and everything used is washed and stored away.

'Once the family's meal has been served, you will again scrub the kitchen passages, kitchen and pantry.

'I know that this is a lot to take in all at once but for the first two days Mary will be on hand to show you what to do, after which she will need to go about her own new duties.' Jennie finally stopped talking.

Poor Maisie felt as though her head would explode with all of this information and she felt tears start to well up in her eyes.

Jennie looked at the little girl sitting there., Poor little thing, this work was going to be hard for her. She gave Maisie a gentle smile. 'You'll be fine, dear, don't worry.' With this she patted Maisie's hand. 'Now go and help Mary with all of those dishes.'

Three Months Later

Maisie felt that she had settled in well. The work was hard but she was well fed and had made good friends with Mary, Peggy and Nancy, although secretly her favourite was Peggy who had a wicked sense of humour.

At night, after all the work was done they would sit together near the kitchen fire and Peggy would relay some of the goings-on in the house, as unlike Maisie, Peggy occasionally got to go upstairs to the family's rooms. She would describe to Maisie what each room looked like and put on a funny high-pitched voice whenever she told stories about Mrs Dean's interactions with the family.

'Oh, our Maze, you should see her, thinks she is part of the gentry, she does. Do this, my girl, or don't do that, girl.' With this last statement her voice was so high that it nearly made her choke. Maisie laughed so hard that tears came to her eyes.

'Peggy, you are awful, don't ever let her catch you,' Maisie pleaded.

'I spoke to Jack earlier, when I went to get some potatoes and he said that he can give us a lift into town and back, but he is leaving early and needs to be back by 2.00 pm. I told him that we only want to get a couple of things and that we promise not to hold him up.' Peggy looked at her little friend. 'Are you all right about going back into the town? I know that you said you were afraid of bumping into your nana, but Jack will be nearby and I know that he won't let anything happen to you.'

Maisie nodded, it was the first day off that she had had in three months and she wanted to enjoy it, but she had a sinking feeling in her stomach that she couldn't explain.

The next morning was bright and sunny and both girls stood in front of Cook, dressed in their Sunday best, although other than their uniforms, these were the only outside clothes they possessed.

'Now, if I let you go you have to promise to behave yourselves. I shall be asking Jack for a report on you.' Cook looked both girls up and down.

'We promise to behave like little ladies.' Peggy put on her funny voice and although Cook didn't want to, it made her laugh.

'Get out of here before I change my mind,' she shouted.

They raced out of the kitchen and across the kitchen courtyard towards the stables, where they found Jack standing solemn faced in the middle of the yard.

'Jack are you all right? What's happened?' asked Peggy,

Jack just shook his head and as he turned away he said, 'You'd better come with me, young Maisie,' and with this he marched back across the kitchen courtyard.

Maisie looked at her friend, who gave her a hug and told her that she had better go. As she entered the kitchen she felt as frightened as she had the first time that she had stepped across the threshold. Jack was in the corner of the kitchen whispering to Cook and as she entered they stopped and looked at her. Cook clicked her tongue in that familiar way that she always did when something had upset her.

'Cook, have I done something wrong?' Maisie was on the verge of tears. 'Please, I haven't done anything.'

'Oh, child, it's not you,' Cook said but her face told Maisie that she was really angry. 'Come with me.'

As they entered the servants' hall Cook said very quietly, 'Don't be afraid, I'll be right here.'

Sitting at the long oak table was her nana. On seeing her, Maisie began to shake. 'Cook please don't let her take me away,' she pleaded.

'Huh, I'm not here to take you away, you stupid girl. I've come to collect my money,' was her nana's curt reply.

Maisie looked from her nana to Cook and back again. 'I don't understand, what money?' She looked at Cook puzzled. 'Please, I don't understand.'

'You've just got paid, haven't you? Well, I expect you to pay up for the board and lodgings that I provided for you after your mother died.' Her nana's voice cut through Maisie like a knife. 'Now, if I've been told correctly your pay for this quarter is two Guineas. That will do nicely for a start.' With this she held out her hand towards Maisie. 'Hurry up and hand it over, girl, I haven't got all day.'

'Please, Nana, I've worked so hard and have been such a good girl, never speaking unless I'm spoken to and never complaining about anything. I need to buy a dress, this one is getting so small for me that I will burst the seams soon. Please don't take my money.' With this she burst into tears.

'Don't waste your tears on me, child, just give me the money and I'll be gone. Well, until next pay day!' With this the old woman stood and started to walk towards the girl, her hand still outstretched. 'You can either give it to me or I will take it.'

'No, you will not.' The voice not only made Maisie jump but stopped her nana in her tracks.

Standing in the doorway was a very elegant lady, dressed exactly the same as Mrs Dean had been the day that Maisie had been taken to her; a black dress with a white lace collar. The only difference was that this lady had a black belt with a very elaborate silver buckle at her waist. She seemed to have an air of nobility about her.

'No-one comes into this house and threatens the staff, however lowly they may be. Now, I think that you had better leave before I call Mr Shore, the under butler, to escort you off the property.' With this she stepped into the room.

The older woman stooped and in a gentler voice proclaimed, 'But I need this money. My husband and I are starving and have no way of making an income. Without this, we will certainly be out on the streets.' She sniffed as if about to cry.

'Nonsense!' Cook, who had been standing quietly outside the doorway in the corridor, bellowed. 'I'm sorry, Miss, but that is nonsense, her husband works at the West End Pit with my older brother. Starving! Look at the size of the woman, she's no more starving than I am.'

On hearing this, Mrs Callow's face darkened. 'I tell you now, girl, that I want that money and I will get it.' Again she advanced towards Maisie.

'I think that you have received enough money already.' Jack burst through the doorway. 'She was paid handsomely for this young thing to come to work here.' With this he stepped forward and grabbed the old lady's arm and dragged her towards the open doorway. 'As the lady has said, do not come back.' With this he gave her an almighty push and to Maisie's relief, she heard her grandmother being shown the door by Jack.

Maisie stood shaking in the corner with huge tears rolling down her face.

'You poor little thing. Go to your room and lie down. I think that you have had enough excitement for one day.' The elegant lady spoke gently to her.

Maisie started towards the door but stopped and turned to the lady, with as deep a curtsy as she could manage and in a very quiet voice she said, 'Thank you, Miss.' With that, she hurried out into the corridor and ran to her room.

The Nursery

Maisie was busy scrubbing the passage between the kitchen and the staff dining room. Although her back felt as though it would break, she was so happy to be living at Wilton Park and she would hum softly to herself as she worked to take her mind off the hard tasks that she had to undertake. She was so busy trying to remove a stain on the tiled floor that she didn't hear someone approaching from behind her.

'Well, what have you been up to, young lady?' came the stern voice of Mrs Dean. The suddenness of her voice made Maisie jump and she dropped the scrubbing brush with a "plop" into the bucket.

Hurriedly she got to her feet and looking down at her boots she whispered, 'Whatever it is, I am very sorry, Mrs Dean. Please don't send me away.' Maisie's days, since that dreadful encounter with her nana, were filled with dread that she would be sent away.

'Whatever it is,' replied Mrs Dean in a mocking tone. 'Well, it had better not be too serious or back to your nana you will go.' With this she looked the girl up and down. 'No, oh, no. This will not do. I can't take you to Miss Brockenhurst looking like that. Follow me and be quick.' With that she turned and marched towards the kitchen.

As she entered the kitchen Maisie heard her shout, 'Bessie! Get here, girl.' She found Bessie standing in front of Mrs Dean and she was visibly shaking.

'I need this one—' with that, she pointed to where Maisie was standing in the doorway, 'To look respectable and it is your duty to make her so, do you understand?'

Bessie nodded her head whilst eyeing the younger girl with a puzzled look on her face.

'Once she is tidy you are to bring her to my room and I don't expect it to take all day. Miss Brockenhurst is expecting us imminently.' Without another word she was gone, leaving Maisie and Bessie staring at each other in bewilderment.

'Oh, Maisie, what have you done?' Bessie asked as she pulled the young girl into the scullery. 'What am I supposed to do to you to make you respectable?' She puzzled for a minute, twisting Maisie this way and that. 'Sit down and let me do your hair.' With this she wet both of her hands in the big enamel sink and started to smooth down Maisie's curls. She then tugged it back into as tight a bun as the thick curls would allow. 'Now wash your hands and face and I'll go and get you a clean apron and cap. Oh, and don't forget to wipe over your boots.'

Maisie was just finishing wiping her face when Bessie returned with the clean items.

'Bessie, who is Miss Brockenhurst?' Maisie felt very scared. 'I really don't know what I have done. I'm sure that I have kept up with all of my chores and I haven't been noisy or broken anything. Oh, Bessie, is she going to send me away?'

Bessie looked into the face of the little girl and her heart went out to her. 'Miss Brockenhurst is the governess to Lady Elizabeth, she is the lady that sent your nana packing the other day and as for sending you away, I doubt it or she would have let your nana have your money. But why she wants to see a little urchin like you is beyond me. You just remember your manners and everything that Jennie has taught you, do you hear me?' With this, Maisie nodded and the two girls headed for Mrs Dean's room.

'Right, come along and no dawdling.' Mrs Dean set off down the corridor. Maisie had never been allowed past the end of the servants' corridor and was amazed at the number of corridors leading off from right and left. How did people remember where to go? she wondered.

Suddenly, on turning a corner they were faced with a very steep set of concrete stairs. Mrs Dean stopped and once again looked Maisie up and down.

'Right, my girl, no speaking unless you are required to,' she snapped. With this she started to climb the steep stairs. At the top of the stairs was a carpeted hallway with five doors leading off it. At the third door Mrs Dean smoothed down her dress and, ensured that her hair was still tightly held back in the bun at the nape of her neck. When she was satisfied that she looked okay she quietly knocked on the door. The door was immediately opened and there stood the elegant lady from the other day.

'Oh, there you are, I was just wondering if you had forgotten.' She addressed this to Mrs Dean. 'I really wanted to talk to you before Lady Elizabeth had woken from her afternoon nap, but never mind, please do come in.'

Maisie found herself standing in the loveliest room that she had ever seen. The walls were adorned with wallpaper featuring little flowers and dotted around them were butterflies. The furniture was upholstered in a lovely red material; the writing desk and small table were both of dark wood. The fire was burning brightly and it gave Maisie a feeling of homeliness. To one side of the room were two doors and through one Maisie could see a room with so many toys that whoever owned it must have bought up the whole of the toy shop.

Mrs Dean's clipped voice suddenly made Maisie's ears prick up. 'Well, Miss Brockenhurst, it would be nice to know why I have had to bring one of my scullery maids away from her chores at a very busy time of day.'

'Why don't we discuss this over a cup of tea?' Miss Brockenhurst indicated the little table set for afternoon tea that stood in front of the fire. 'Please do sit down, Mrs Dean. Maisie, sit over there on the chair near the window.' Maisie did as she was told and sat as Jennie had taught her, with her feet together and her hands on her lap.

Once the tea was poured, Miss Brockenhurst started to talk.

'After that terrible incident with Mrs Callow the other day and after meeting Maisie—' with this she turned slightly and gave the young girl a little smile, 'She is such a polite girl and as you say, a very hard worker— well, I started to think about her situation and after speaking to Lady Willaby, I have come up with a solution that should work out very nicely for all of us.'

Mrs Dean almost choked on her tea. 'You spoke to Lady Willaby about this urchin?' she spluttered.

'Yes, Mrs Dean, I most certainly did and she has agreed with my plan,' came the indignant reply. 'From tomorrow, Maisie will come to work in the nursery, where she will help Nurse with Lady Elizabeth's needs. She will do the fetching and carrying but will also be a young companion for Lady Elizabeth, who misses having someone of her own age around the place. It really is no fun for her, playing on her own every day. Maisie can move her belongings into the bedroom at the end of the hallway so that she is available to help at any time of the day or night.'

'Well, I don't know. I have far more experienced girls that surely would be better suited to mix with the upper house than this one.' With that, she cast a dismissive hand in Maisie's direction. 'After all, she has only been here for a short period of time and really doesn't have the finesse to be part of the upper house.'

Maisie could tell from the tone of Mrs Dean's voice that she was not happy. Maisie was quite bemused by what she had just heard and wasn't really sure what it all meant, but she remained sitting quietly just as Jennie had told her to do.

'You are of course entitled to your opinion, Mrs Dean, but it is Maisie whom both Lady Willaby and I wish to work here in the nursery. If you are worried about the chores, then please do not be. Mrs Crisp will be coming to work in the kitchen on the days that she is not doing the laundry. Since her husband died she needs the extra money and is happy to take on the work that Maisie would have done.'

'Well, it seems to me that everything is settled without any input from me,' came the hostile reply. 'After all, I am just the housekeeper, who supposedly is in charge of the female staff. It would have been nice to have been given this information before the final decision was made.'

'I am sure that if you are unhappy about any of this, Lady Willaby would be only too happy to hear your concerns.' Miss Brockenhurst put down her cup and saucer. 'Would you like me to make an appointment for you to see her?'

'No, no, it won't be necessary,' came the speedy reply.

'Right. Now that has been settled, I will expect Maisie to move her belongings into her room before Lady Elizabeth has her tea.' With this Miss Brockenhurst stood, indicating that the meeting was over.

Once at the bottom of the steep staircase, Mrs Dean turned to Maisie and in a very angry whisper, she said, 'If you ever tell anyone that I knew nothing about this matter, I swear I will ensure that you are back with your nana. Now go to your room and collect the few things that you have and go straight back up to the nursery.' With that she turned on her heel and marched off down the corridor.

The Meeting

Maisie woke with a start and sat bolt upright in bed. Looking around her new room, she gave herself a little hug. 'Oh, thank goodness, it wasn't a dream.' She smiled as she spoke to herself. She had never had a room all to herself and this one was truly lovely. The walls were painted in a cream colour and she had a little dressing table, although she had nothing to put in it. In one corner was a small wardrobe; she had carefully hung her best, and only, dress and shawl in there last night. A mirror was fixed to the wall above her wash table, which had a plain white bowl and jug standing on it. She was still sitting admiring her room when a quiet knock on the door jolted her back to reality.

The door slowly opened and standing there was Peggy. 'Good Morning, Miss.' She gave a little curtsy and started to giggle. 'I have your hot water here.' With this she crossed the room to the wash stand and tipped the hot water into the jug. 'I like your room, it's very nice. Maisie, you make sure that you behave yourself, but don't forget to come and see us when you can.'

'Peggy, I don't understand. Why are you bringing me water?' Maisie shook her head as if to clear her thoughts. 'What is going on?'

Peggy peered through the open door to ensure that no-one was in the hallway and then came over and sat on the edge of the bed. 'Maisie, you are very lucky that Miss Brockenhurst thinks that you have the making of a companion for Lady Elizabeth. She can see in you what we all have since you arrived. You are different from the rest of us, Maisie. I can't tell you what it is but there is just something about you. Make the most of this opportunity, listen carefully and you will learn much.' With this she gave her a little peck on the cheek. 'See you tomorrow, Miss.

At this, Maisie threw her pillow at her. 'Get out of here,' she laughed.

After washing in the hot water, Maisie pulled on her bonnet and apron and started about what she thought would be her duties. She crossed the hallway and started to ensure that the fire in the sitting room was stacked properly and that the log bin, which stood next to the fire grate, was full.

'Oh, Maisie, that is no longer your job.' Miss Brockenhurst's kind voice came from behind her.

'Sorry, Miss, but I'm not quite sure what my duties are,' Maisie stuttered, standing up quickly and smoothing down her apron.

'Don't worry, as soon as Nurse Black gets here all will become clear,' came the reply as the older woman crossed the room and sat herself next to the fire, where her breakfast had been laid on the little oak table.

'Did I hear my name being mentioned?' came a slightly high-pitched voice from the hallway. 'I hope that there's a cup of tea waiting for me.'

Miss Brockenhurst laughed. 'Of course, dear Mary, isn't there always?' With this, the door to the sitting room was pushed open and in walked a very matronly looking woman. She was about five feet tall with a round face that was accentuated by her hair being tightly pulled back in a very tight bun. She wore a dark blue dress and a heavy blue cloak, which was tied with a bow at her neck.

As she entered the room she was also laughing. 'And a nice piece of toast, I hope.' She stopped short on seeing Maisie standing next to the fire. 'Oh, so this is the young lady I have heard so much about. But you do know, Hope, that this will not do,' she pointed at Maisie's uniform. 'Not here in the nursery.'

Miss Brockenhurst laughed. 'I thought a trip down to the basement storage after breakfast, there are a lot of dresses and uniforms stored there from when the children were very small. We should be able to find something.' Turning to Maisie, she said, 'Go to the kitchen and get some breakfast, but be back here in half an hour. You have a lot to learn today.'

Maisie backed out of the room and at the doorway, bobbed a curtsy to the two older women. Turning on her heel she sped through the long corridors until she reached the passage leading to the kitchen. 'Right, Maisie girl, deep breath,' she said to herself as she made sure that her clothes and hair were straight. The familiar hum of voices echoed into the passage from the servants' hall and she could hear the sound of talking coming from the kitchen.

Sitting at the far end of the kitchen at the little round table were Jennie, Cook and Bessie. All three fell quiet as she entered.

'Ah, here's our little lady,' said Cook with a smile on her face. 'Breakfast is served.' With this Bessie got up and in a very elaborate gesture, brushed the remaining empty seat with a cloth and gave a deep curtsy.

'Stop it,' Maisie chided as she took her seat, and all four companions started to laugh.

'I can't believe what is happening to me,' Maisie informed the others. 'Do any of you know what on earth is going on?'

'I overheard Mrs Dean talking to Mr Shore, the butler. She wasn't very happy, going on and on she was about how unfair it was that some silly little urchin of a girl would be mingling with the upper house,' Jennie stated with a smile. 'It's about time someone got the better of her.'

'Now, Jennie, you be careful what you say,' Cook interrupted her. As she did she bent slightly to one side and peered through the open kitchen door. 'Walls have ears, dear.' With that she nodded her head and put her finger up to her lips.

After a hearty breakfast of thick sliced bacon, egg and toast Maisie made her way back through the corridors towards the nursery. As she rounded a corner she nearly collided with Miss Brockenhurst, who was coming in the opposite direction.

'Oh, Miss, I am so sorry, am I late?' enquired Maisie.

'No, not at all,' came the reply. 'I thought that we could go straight down to the basement to hopefully find you some more fitting clothes.'

Maisie dutifully followed. She had never been down into the basement before and was amazed at the number of doors leading off the concrete passageway. After passing the first two or three Miss Brockenhurst suddenly stopped and reaching into her pocket, brought out a bunch of keys. After trying several the big wooden door started to open and there in front of Maisie was rail after rail of clothing, some covered by thick sheets. The older woman walked across to the opposite side of the room and pulled back a heavy curtain. Although the window close to the ceiling was fairly small, the room was suddenly filled with sunlight. Miss Brockenhurst moved from rail to rail, muttering to herself as she went until finally, 'Ah, here they are.' With that she pulled the heavy sheeting from the rail and started sorting through the clothes.

'Come here, Maisie,' she called over her shoulder. 'Let me see if these will fit you.'

As each item was held up against Maisie it would either be hung back on the rail or placed on a chair next to it. After about half an hour Miss Brockenhurst gave a satisfied sigh. 'Now then, we must get Mrs Jones to make some alterations. She needs to take off all of the lace – a girl of your age should not be seen in lace – and take the hems up a little.' She carried on, mostly to herself, 'A cape is what we need, where on earth are all of the outside garments?' She busied herself again from rail to rail and then, spotting a large trunk in the corner, called Maisie over to help her with the lid.

Maisie's head was still reeling, she couldn't believe that all of the dresses and petticoats on the chair were for her and now a cape as well. She'd only ever owned one decent dress and a raggedy knitted shawl that didn't keep any of the cold out.

'Maisie, stop day dreaming,' came the stern voice. 'Let me see if this fits you.' Miss Brockenhurst was holding up a dark blue cape in heavy wool, which she threw around the young girl's shoulders. 'Right, that's the lot for now. I need you to take all of this over to Mrs Jones. I will write a note for you to take so that she will understand exactly what is needed.'

Maisie struggled under the weight of the clothes that she was carrying, but was far too happy to let Miss Brockenhurst see. After they had made their way back to the nursery, Miss Brockenhurst sat at her desk and started to write. On finishing she folded the paper over and handed this to Maisie. As she did so Nurse Black entered the room followed by a gangly young lad who, Maisie guessed, was a few years older than her. He looked out of place in the nursery and seemed very nervous.

'Oh, good, there you are, Tom. I need you to help Maisie carry these clothes over to your mother. Now, Maisie, don't be all day, as soon as Mrs Jones has measured you I expect you to come straight back.

Maisie nodded and started to collect the items of clothing. Seeing this, Tom stepped forward.

'Let me carry these, Miss, they look far too heavy for a little thing like you.'

Once outside in the courtyard Maisie looked at her young companion; he was indeed older than her, she would guess, at about sixteen with thick unruly blond hair and a lopsided grin. 'What you staring at?' he stuttered. He was walking so fast that poor Maisie had a job to keep up with him.

'Can you slow down a bit?' she panted. 'Not all of us have such long legs, you know, and I wasn't staring, I was looking.'

Stopping, he turned to look at her. 'You're the girl that my dad brought up from the town, the one that her grandma sold.'

'Oh, does everyone know that I wasn't wanted by my own family?' Maisie's eyes filled with tears and at that moment all of the joy of her new clothes vanished.

'I'm sorry, I didn't mean to be unkind. My ma is always telling me that I should think before I open my big stupid mouth.' As he spoke he dropped his head. 'Really, I didn't mean to upset you.'

Maisie's heart went out to him, he looked so forlorn. 'Don't worry, it's the truth and anyway, if she hadn't sold me I wouldn't have all these lovely new clothes.' With this she gave a little laugh. 'We best get moving, otherwise I'll be in trouble with Miss Brockenhurst'

Raising his head, he nodded and started off towards a cottage next to the stable block, with Maisie trotting behind him.

Mrs Jones was tall and thin, with a thick mop of blond hair which was escaping from the bun fastened at her neck. She looked up and smiled as the two entered the cottage. 'Well, I've been waiting to meet you, Jack has told me all about you. Would you like a cup of tea?' Without waiting for Maisie's reply she instructed Tom to put the kettle on. 'Now then, let's see what she has found for you.' After sorting through the pile of clothes and giving Maisie the once over she sat herself down opposite Maisie.

'Well, how do you like living in the big house, my dear? Are they being kind to you?'

'Oh yes, I have no complaints, although the last few days have been a bit of a surprise.' Maisie sipped her tea. 'I'm not sure why I have been chosen to work in the nursery.'

Mrs Jones placed her cup on the little table beside her. 'My dear, I think that I know. They can see something in you that the others don't have, I guess you would say a kind of yearning. Now, young lady, off you go. I will get these done double quick so that you can get out of that drab uniform. Once I've finished, Tom here,' she gestured to her son, 'can bring them over. It was nice to meet you and if you ever want a cup of tea or an ear to talk to, you know where I am.'

With that, Maisie thanked the older woman and made her way back towards the big house and the nursery.

Lady Elizabeth

Today was the first day that she would meet Lady Elizabeth. The previous evening Miss Brockenhurst had sat Maisie down in front of the fire in the little sitting room. 'As you know you will meet Lady Elizabeth tomorrow so I want to tell you a little about her so that you will not be shocked.' Miss Brockenhurst had a very solemn expression which bothered Maisie. 'Two years ago, when she was out riding with Lord Philip she fell from her pony and unfortunately, since then she has not been able to walk unaided.' At this she fell silent. After a while she continued. 'She can sometimes be spiteful, but this is due to her frustration at not being able to do things for herself. If she is mean to you, bear in mind what she has lost.'

'Will she be very mean to me?' Maisie was very troubled by this new information. 'Will she hit me?'

'Oh, Maisie, I hope not, but Nurse Black and I have both had objects thrown at us. Luckily they have missed. Mainly it is her tongue that she uses to say mean things.' She shook her head slightly. 'Now go to bed, as tomorrow will be very busy.'

Maisie stood in her bedroom. Her heart was thumping and she had butterflies in her stomach. For the hundredth time that morning she practised her curtsy. She smoothed down the pale green dress, which Mrs Jones had altered for her; this was to be her new uniform. Nurse Black had told her that when they were attending to Lady Elizabeth in the nursery, a crisp white apron must be worn at all times.

'Come on, Maisie girl, you don't want to be late, that won't do.' Maisie spoke to her reflection in the little mirror above her wash stand.

She joined Nurse Black in the sitting room. After she had been checked over to make sure that she was presentable, Nurse Black led her from the room and down the corridor. At a big, white wooden door Nurse Black stopped and tentatively knocked. A faint sound could be heard from within. Without looking round Nurse Black whispered, 'Into the lion's den we go.'

The room was nothing like Maisie had expected. It was very "girly", with pink walls and butterflies and fairies painted in delicate colours on the walls. Two large windows faced the door and sitting between them was a beautiful white and gold chest of drawers with two ballerina figures adorning the top. To the right of the door was a huge dolls' house, the biggest Maisie had ever seen. Next to that were various dolls sitting around a little table as if having a tea party. To the left of the door was a wash stand and at the far end of the room was a big white four-poster bed.

Maisie followed Nurse Black and stood to the side of the bed. Lying there was the prettiest little girl; surely this wasn't the dragon that they had been warning her about? Maisie thought that she must be about thirteen years old. She had blond hair that was escaping from under her night cap.

'Good Morning, Lady Elizabeth.' Nurse Black spoke she bobbed a curtsy; Maisie followed suit. 'This is Maisie, who we have spoken about.' She nodded her head in Maisie's direction. 'Are you ready to get up?'

Two very blue eyes suddenly flew open. 'Well, I think that you should have waited to bring this girl in until I was washed and dressed,' came the haughty reply. 'After all, I am at a bit of disadvantage, don't you think?'

At this, Nurse Black's face went very red and Maisie couldn't tell if this was from embarrassment or anger. 'Would you like me to send her away? She can wait in the nursery if you would prefer.'

'Yes, indeed I would prefer,' she snapped. Her eyes closed again and Maisie hurried from the room.

Miss Brockenhurst was setting up a table when Maisie entered the nursery.

'Why aren't you with Nurse Black? Oh, my goodness, what have you done?'

'Nothing, I haven't done anything. Lady Elizabeth wasn't happy that I was there.' Maisie recounted the whole conversation. At the end Miss Brockenhurst tutted. 'Should I go back to the kitchen?' Maisie asked. She was very unhappy that the first meeting had gone so badly.

'No, no. Everything will be fine. I expect she was just a bit unnerved at having someone else there as soon as she awoke.' But from the worried look on the governess's face, Maisie wasn't so sure.

After about an hour, Nurse Black wheeled the young girl into the nursery.

'Come here and stand in front of me.' she commanded Maisie. 'As you would have guessed by now, I am not a morning person and I certainly do not like surprises so early in the morning.' At this she shot a very dark look at the poor nurse. 'Now then, tell me all about yourself. I have been told certain things but I want to hear it from you.'

After Maisie had explained how she had come to live at the hall and about her nana's visit she fell quiet.

'Good, at least you appear to be honest, so you can stay.' She had a way of speaking that was very matter-of-fact and sounded far too old for her age. 'For the time being,' she suddenly added.

However, after this first encounter everything seemed to settle down and on the whole the two girls seemed to get on reasonably well. Lady Elizabeth would correct Maisie's grammar but in a very kind way and to everyone's surprise, Maisie would make Lady Elizabeth laugh with silly anecdotes from when she was living with her mammy or nana. The only time that Maisie would fall quiet was if she was asked about her little sisters. She still had no idea what had happened to her three sisters and this was a cause of great sadness for Maisie. She knew that the only person who knew was her nana and there was no way that she would tell her, especially after been shown the door by Miss Brockenhurst.

At first Maisie would stand to one side when Lady Elizabeth had her lessons with Miss Brockenhurst in the nursery, in case refreshments were needed. However, on one particular day, as Maisie handed Lady Elizabeth her lesson book a sudden thought came into the girl's head.

'I'm sure that it would be beneficial to Maisie if she were allowed to join in. After all, she's not needed for anything else whilst I am tortured by my lessons.' This was addressed to a startled Miss Brockenhurst.

'Well, I suppose no harm can come of it,' she answered cautiously. 'After all, as you quite rightly point out this could prove of benefit not only to Maisie, but to the house as well. Would you like to join in?' This was added as she turned in Maisie's direction.

'Oh, yes, Miss. I would very much but I don't want to be a nuisance or get in the way of Lady Elizabeth's lessons,' came the timid reply.

And so Maisie's education started. She found that she loved the reading and writing lessons but found that maths was not one of her great subjects, but over the coming weeks and months she began to find that it wasn't so hard after all and was soon able to calculate quite complicated equations better than Lady Elizabeth. Miss Brockenhurst, at times, could not hide her surprise at how quickly Maisie seemed to be able to pick things up and decided that it would be a good idea to allow her to also join in with the French lessons that Lady Elizabeth had reluctantly agreed to try.

The months rolled by and soon the summer was upon them. The two girls liked nothing better than to go out into the grounds and find somewhere warm but shaded to draw. The two footmen, Chris Brown and Dan O'Brien, would come to the nursery and carry Lady Elizabeth down to the ground floor, where she would sit and wait for them to fetch her bath chair. They would then push her to the chosen spot, returning occasionally to enquire if lemonade or refreshments were needed. Maisie loved these times as she had found that she had quite a flair for drawing and had completed several pictures that now adorned her bedroom walls.

The Copse

Hope Brockenhurst settled herself in the window seat of her room. From this position, she could enjoy the sunshine and also keep an eye on Lady Elizabeth and Maisie, who had taken their drawing materials and were sitting in the shade under the big oak tree at the edge of the little copse that ran along the edge of the lawn.

It was lovely to see the two young girls getting on so well and Hope marvelled at the way that Maisie had adjusted to life upstairs, she was a real treasure. With Maisie as her companion Lady Elizabeth had started to blossom.

Hope was suddenly jolted out of her day dream by what sounded like a dreadful commotion at the front of the house. Leaning forward, she saw three young men strolling across the lawn towards where the girls were sitting, they were laughing loudly and jostling with each other. She realised that it was Lord Phillip and his two young gentlemen companions, who had all arrived the previous evening from their boarding school down in Dorset. There was something in the way that they were acting that suddenly made her feel very uneasy.

She watched as the three approached the young girls and was shocked at what happened next. Lord Phillip grabbed Maisie's arm and pulled her to her feet, almost throwing her into the waiting arms of his companions. It looked to Hope as though he was saying something to Lady Elizabeth, who had dropped her drawing materials and had her head in her hands. As she watched, the other two began to drag Maisie into the copse. Lord Phillip turned and quickly followed his companions.

Hope screamed as she realised what was happening and gathering her skirts, she ran as fast as she could along the top floor corridor and down the four flights of stairs. Although her lungs felt as if they would burst she knew that she could not stop; she prayed that she did not bump into any of the members of the family and that the staff would all be below stairs.

At last she reached the front door. As she raced down the stone steps she caught a glimpse of young Tom coming around the side of the house. Without stopping she shouted to him, 'Quickly, quickly, come with me.' She rushed forward across the lawn. Tom had never seen one of the upper house ladies run, but he only needed to take one look at her anxious face to know that something dreadful must have happened; he raced behind her without any questions.

Inside the copse Maisie was terrified. She had no idea of the fate that these three young gentlemen had planned for her.

'Please, sir, I'm a good girl. Please don't hurt me.'

'Hear that, boys? This little slut is a good girl.' Lord Phillip made an elaborate bow. 'Now, where do we start, at the top or the bottom?' He looked her up and down. As he approached the struggling Maisie, the look on his face made the girl even more afraid. 'For god's sake hold still.' Bringing his hand back, he hit her hard across the face. The force of the blow had the desired effect of stunning Maisie and she slumped forward.

The three young men were so intent on achieving their mission to deflower Maisie that they did not notice the tall dark shadow of a man standing in the bushes.

As Lord Phillip started to unbutton Maisie's bodice, Hope and Tom came crashing through the undergrowth.

'STOP! Don't you dare go any further,' Hope shouted. The three boys all jumped at the sudden interruption, looking at Maisie who was still slumped between the two boys, her arms being tightly held behind her back. Hope said as strongly as her lungs would allow, 'Let her go, now.'

'Or what?' came the haughty reply from the young lord. 'You are nothing but a servant and cannot tell me what to do. If I want to get to know this,' he pointed to Maisie, 'then I shall.' He stepped forward as if to carry on unbuttoning her bodice.

'I think that you had better let the young lady go,' a deep rasping voice stated as the man stepped from the bushes. He was dressed completely in black with a big black cape and had the hood pulled down over his face. In his right hand he held a long thick pole and his left hand was clenched into a tight fist.

The three young men froze.

'Who the hell are you?' stammered Edward, the smallest of the three.

'No matter, just do as I say and no-one will get hurt. Take her now.' This was directed at Hope. Tom ran forward and gathered Maisie up in his arms. 'Make sure she's okay and I will deal with these three scoundrels.' The man lowered his head further as if thinking. 'Yes, indeed I will deal with these three.'

Tom carefully carried the dazed girl out of the copse and slowly and gently set her down on the blanket next to Lady Elizabeth. Once he was sure that she was all right he stood and looking at Hope, asked, 'What do you think he meant by dealing with them?' Rubbing his chin, he continued, 'You don't think that he is going to, you know—' he nodded in a very adult way. 'Maybe we should check to make sure exactly what he meant.'

Hope, was also quite concerned. She had never come across anything like it before. However reluctant she was to leave the two girls alone and go back into the copse, she also felt that maybe they should go and check exactly what the man meant. Ensuring that the two girls were all right and instructing them to stay together, Tom and Hope made their way carefully and quietly back into the copse.

Tom stood open-mouthed, looking at the sight in front of them. In the very spot that they had decided was a good place to strip Maisie, they themselves had been stripped naked. With their hands and feet bound they had been rendered completely defenceless. 'Don't just stand there, you idiot, help us,' screamed Lord Phillip.

'Oh, my goodness!' Hope burst out laughing at the three naked young men. 'What have we here? Oh, dear, did he take your fine clothes? Well, I hope that you can all run very fast, as I do not think that Lady Willaby will be very amused at three naked young gentlemen walking across her lawn.'

'You can't leave us like this,' sobbed Henry; he was the tallest of the boys.

'And how exactly was Maisie going to be left?' asked Hope. 'I'm sure that you weren't going to give her back all of her clothes.' She started to turn away. 'But for the sake of the other ladies of the house, I suppose that for decency we cannot let you walk around completely naked.' Addressing Tom, she continued, 'Would you please go to the stables and bring three horse blankets for these fine young gentlemen, but please ensure that they are NOT clean.' With this she gave him a little smile. 'Oh, and Tom – no need to hurry. I think that these gentlemen need a little time to reflect on their actions.' With that the two of them started back through the undergrowth towards the lawn. Hope suddenly stopped and turned back to the three who were still lying on the ground.

'Gentlemen, if I were you I would stay very quiet and still. I heard that the groundsmen are culling wild hogs today and your sobbing sounds remarkably like the sound that dirty little hogs make.' Turning on her heel, she slowly walked away.

As they entered the nursery, Maisie was still shaking. 'Why would they do that to me, Miss? I'm a good girl. I didn't encourage them, I promise,' she sobbed.

'Now, now dear, it's okay. I saw what happened from the window here.' Hope nodded towards the window seat. 'If anyone will be in trouble, it certainly will not be you.'

'My brother and his friends always cause trouble when they come to stay. I hate it when I know he is on his way home, especially when he brings friends with him.' Lady Elizabeth stroked Maisie's hand gently. 'Don't worry, Maisie. I won't let anything happen to you.'

Maisie buried her head in her hands. Suddenly, she looked up at her two companions and with a startled expression, asked, 'Who was that man? Did he come into the copse with you?' She looked at Hope, who shook her head; she had been wondering the very same thing.

Later that evening, 'Right then,' Cook said to Chris Brown, one of the younger footmen. 'Make sure that you carry this carefully, I don't want any slippage.' Cook had been presented by the head groundsman, as was the tradition, with the first kill of the day; a lovely succulent piglet. She had spent most of the day ensuring that it was cooked to perfection for the master's dinner and it was now laid out on a silver platter with the traditional apple placed in its mouth. She had placed roast potatoes, boiled potatoes and broccoli around the piglet and even though she said so herself, it looked fit for a king.

Mr Shore walked in front of Chris Brown and as they entered the dining room, where the family plus the two young guests and Hope Brockenhurst were seated, he announced the arrival of the pig, as was the custom of the first kill. They all clapped as the footman brought the piglet to the table and laid it carefully in front of the master.

Lord Willaby was just about to start carving the piglet when Lady Elizabeth burst into laughter. 'Oh, my goodness. How appropriate,' she stated, looking at the three young men, who had all turned a very bright shade of red.

'Elizabeth, what is the meaning of this?' came an angry demand from her father, as he looked from Elizabeth to his son, who was unable to make eye contact with him.

'Please excuse me, it's just that suddenly something from earlier today jumped into my head. I am truly very sorry,' came the meek reply.

'Is this how a young lady should behave at the table?' Lord Willaby stood, eyes blazing, looking around the table until they came to rest on his wife.

'My dear, I think that this is something that I will discuss with Elizabeth after our meal,' stated Lady Willaby and looking at the three young men, 'and that you, dear, should fully discuss with these three when you all retire to your study. Now, that piglet looks and smells delicious, shall we eat?'

When the master and the three young gentlemen retired to the master's study, Chris Brown, as usual, hurried to get the fine port from the cellar. The master always enjoyed a port or two after dinner. As normal he stopped outside the master's study to ensure that the tray and himself were presented properly. He had just been about to knock when he heard the

Lord Willaby explode with rage; he had never heard Lord Willaby shout before.

'Sirs, you are both stupid and disrespectful and I will not have such people in my house. Tomorrow morning, I will get Jack to drive you back into town where you will catch the train back to Dorset. As for you, Phillip, until you can behave yourself as a gentleman you will spend holidays with Uncle Ralph on Portland. Close your mouth, sir. Don't you dare say a word to me.'

Cook and Jennie had just settled themselves at the little table in the corner of the kitchen to enjoy a peaceful breakfast, when the big wooden back door flew open and Peggy came rushing in.

'For goodness' sake, girl, is the house on fire?' Cook was a bit irritated as she had a nice piece of bacon waiting to be eaten.

'Have you heard?' shouted Peggy as she raced across the kitchen towards the two of them.

'What are you talking about now, Peggy? Come and sit down and have your breakfast, I'm sure it's not that important.' Cook started to cut her bacon and Jennie continued to butter her toast; they knew how Peggy got excited over nothing.

'No, really, Cook, Chris Brown told me.'

Both of the older woman looked at each other and back at Peggy.

'He said that there was a terrible row in the master's study after dinner last night, something about the copse and a dark man. Apparently, the young masters are all being sent packing today, back down to Dorset—' Peggy stopped for breath. 'But the strangest thing of all was when Mrs Crisp went out to scrub the front steps this morning, there, laid out as neat as you like, was three sets of gentlemen's clothing, including their undergarments.' At this she blushed and tried hard to stifle a giggle.

Cook, who had been listening to this with her fork halfway up to her mouth, and Jennie, who was sitting open-mouthed, looked at each other.

'Well, what a carry on,' said Cook. 'I wonder if Maisie knows any further details. We must ask her when she comes down for her breakfast.'

But Maisie didn't come down for breakfast, or any other meal after that.

The Fair

As normal, Peggy brought the hot water for Maisie to wash but today she was all of a flutter.

'Whatever is the matter with you, Peggy Skiffins?' chided Maisie. 'That's the third time you've admired yourself in the mirror.'

Peggy's cheeks flushed. 'I think I've got me a suitor,' she stammered.

'You only think that you have, don't you know?' The teasing just made Peggy go redder.

'Well, you know that the August Fair is coming to town? Well, I've been asked by someone if I'm going and when I said I didn't know, he said that the fair wouldn't be the same if I wasn't there.' With this she gave her friend a little shy smile. 'So I take it that he must be a bit sweet on me.'

'Oh, my sweet Peggy, who is this lucky man then? Does he have a name?' Maisie tickled Peggy under the chin. 'Or is he a figment of your imagination, young Peggy?'

'No, he's not and if you must know, it's Brian Henasey. He works with the groundsmen and sometimes in the stables.' She was still blushing. 'I think he's very handsome in a funny sort of way.'

'So will you be going with Mr Henasey then? Only I was hoping that if we get some time off, we might go together.'

Maisie felt a bit let down as she and Peggy always spent their one day off a month together.

'The thing is, I can't be seen to be with him on my own as, Mrs Dean would have my guts for garters. You know what she's like about us having visitors and I'm not sure it would be right to be in town on my own when the fair's here. You know what they say about the girls that hang around the travellers. I don't want to be tarred with that brush, thank you very much.'

'So, what you are really saying is that you want me to act as your chaperone?' Maisie hugged her friend. 'If that's the only way I can go to the fair then it's a deal. You tell your Mr Henasey that he owes me a lemonade.'

Peggy hugged her back. 'Now all we have to hope is that Mrs Dean and Miss Brockenhurst give us the same time off.' With that, Peggy went on her way.

Thursday morning in the servants' quarters, everyone was buzzing. They had all had permission to go into town to the fair. The younger ones were allowed to go in the day and the older servants in the evening. They had all been given a very strict talk to by Mr Shore and Mrs Dean. If anyone came back worse for drink they would be out on their ear and as for the younger ones, if they caused any trouble in the town the same fate waited for them.

By the time that Jack brought the big open wagon round to the kitchen door, the excitement had mounted to such a pitch that Mrs Dean had threatened not to let the young ones go. Immediately they all shut up and she went back into the house, muttering about how no good would come of this day.

Maisie sat next to Peggy and whispered, 'Well, where is he then?'

Peggy blushed. 'He's already in town. He didn't have to come to work at all today.'

The wagon slowly made its way along the winding roads. Every time that Maisie travelled into town she thought of that first journey and how frightened she had been. As if reading her mind, Jack turned slightly in his seat and smiled at her.

By the time they arrived the town was full and Jack had a job steering the horse and wagon through the throngs of excited people. He had never seen it so busy this early in the day, but he supposed that as it was a sunny day more people had ventured out. He pulled on the reins and the wagon came to a shuddering halt.

'Now then, you lot, I will be leaving here at exactly 5.00 pm. If you're not here I'm not waiting. Go on then, get lost, the lot of you,' he laughed and they all excitedly clambered down the rickety steps of the wagon.

The two girls linked arms and skipped down the street towards the fair. Neither one of them noticed the old lady watching them.

'Well, well, if it's not our fine lady Maisie,' murmured Mrs Callow. 'Let's see if you're still laughing by the end of the day.' With that she took a long, slow swig of her beer, wiping the froth from her mouth with the back of her hand as she started to formulate her plan.

The girls had been at the fair for about an hour when suddenly in front of them, cap in hand, stood Peggy's young suitor. 'Can I buy you both a lemonade or ice cream?' the young man stammered. His cheeks were very red and he kept turning his cap around in his hands. Maisie felt very sorry for him; it had obviously taken a lot of courage for him to approach them.

Peggy giggled. 'Oh, thank you. A lemonade would be nice. This is my friend Maisie.' She turned slightly in Maisie's direction without taking her eyes off the young man's face.

Brian gave a slight bow. 'Nice to meet you, Miss.' He was surprised that Peggy had a friend who obviously was quite well off, if the clothes she was wearing had anything to do with it.

'And it's very nice to meet you too, Mr Henasey.' Maisie took in the appearance of the young man. He was short and stocky with a mop of ginger hair, not at all the type that she thought would have appealed to Peggy, but he did have a very nice smile and dancing green eyes. 'Please don't waste your money on a drink for me, I really am not that thirsty.' Maisie was sure that he didn't have too much money and wanted him to enjoy the time that he had with Peggy. 'You two go ahead, I just want to watch the carousel for a while. I'll just sit here under this tree in the shade.'

'I'm not sure that we should leave you on your own.' Peggy looked very worried. 'Cook said to stay together.'

'Don't worry, I promise I won't move and if anyone comes near I'll scream so loud that the whole town will hear me. Now go and have your lemonade, I'm sure that Brian would like some time with you alone.' Maisie winked at her friend. 'But Peggy, be back within the hour.'

Without any further hesitation Peggy hurried over to where Brian was waiting for her. Maisie smiled as she watched them go; she felt like a proud mother.

After a while Maisie started to feel quite sleepy. She wasn't sure if it was the warmth of the late summer sun or if it was watching the carousel go round and round that was making her eyelids droop but she was finding it extremely difficult to stay awake.

'Here, drink this.' A cup of what looked like water was being thrust at Maisie. She looked up to see a tall, dark-haired boy standing in front of her. 'You looked as though you were about to faint, you've most probably been sitting there too long in the sun, this will make you feel better.' He had an unusual accent that Maisie couldn't make out. She did feel very hot and took the drink and gratefully drank. It tasted bitter and made Maisie want to gag.

'What is it? I thought you were giving me water.' She struggled with her words and then to her dismay started to giggle.

'I never said it was water, I said it would make you feel better and if I'm not mistaken, what with your laughing and all, it's done the trick,' the boy answered. As he did so he looked past her and seemed to nod his head.

Suddenly from nowhere a hand clamped across Maisie's mouth and a large dirty arm folded around her waist, 'If you know what's best for you, you won't struggle,' a deep growling voice spoke in Maisie's ear. 'Come on, boy, hurry up and get the wagon door open.' The man frogmarched the frightened girl quickly down a side alley where a large wagon stood. The boy said something to the man and they both laughed. Maisie was bundled into the wagon and was hauled towards the back, behind some bales of hay.

'Now then, boy, get her hands and feet tied and make sure they're tied tightly. This will do for a gag.' With that the man threw a piece of cloth onto the floor next to the boy, who was already busy tying Maisie up.

'Please tell me what is happening! Why are you doing this to me?' She looked directly into the boy's eyes, who seemed to be struggling to look at her.

'Just shut up, stay quiet and he won't get mad.' He glanced over his shoulder at the man who was now standing outside of the wagon talking to someone. From Maisie's position she couldn't see who it was but was sure that it was a woman's voice she could hear.

'Come on, boy, what's taking you so long? We've got work to do.' With that the young lad hurried towards the open door and jumped down from the wagon, the big door was slammed shut and Maisie heard the bolt being rammed into place.

What was to become of her? She sat in the damp, dark wagon and wept as she had never wept before.

After what seemed like hours, she heard the man and boy talking.

'Get in the wagon, whilst I speak to this one.' Movement of the wagon told her that the boy had jumped up in front. 'Well, what do I get for giving you a lift?' The man had a leery sound to his voice as he spoke.

Laughing, the woman, who to Maisie sounded very young, replied, 'Well, then, I think that you already know how I make my living and pays my bills.'

'If I'm going a mile out of my way it had better be worth it.' After that there was no more conversation and the wagon began to jolt forward over the uneven cobblestones of the alleyway.

Some time later the wagon stopped and Maisie could hear the young woman and the man in what sounded like a heated argument.

'What do you mean, I don't get any cause' I won't drive right up to your door?' A heavy thud against the side of the wagon made Maisie jump. The man started to curse under his breath and from the groans that could be heard, it sounded to the girl as if he was lifting something heavy.

'Oh, my god. What have you been and done?' This was the young boy's voice and from where Maisie lay in the back of the wagon, he sounded very afraid.

'Get back in the wagon and stay put while I deal with this.' The man's voice sounded very laboured. 'If anyone comes by you tell 'em that I've gone for a slash, do you understand?' Without waiting, the sound of heavy footsteps could be heard retreating into the distance.

Maisie was sure that she heard crying from the front of the wagon. Suddenly, without warning the wagon again lurched forward and the journey continued.

The Search

Maisie woke up with a jolt. Her mouth was dry and her head was banging. Looking around, she suddenly remembered what had happened. Tears welled up in her already swollen eyes. What was to become of her? As the wagon swayed from side to side as it went down what could only be a very bumpy road, she could hear the clatter of metal on metal but was unsure what it was. Her limbs were cramped and she felt dirty, uncomfortable and very afraid.

Suddenly the wagon came to a creaking halt and she could hear men's voices shouting, but couldn't hear what was being said. She was suddenly aware of someone walking along the side of the wagon and the bolt on the back door being moved. The large doors opened and light streamed in from the outside.

'Get in there and bring her out and don't take all day.' This was the voice of the big man who had kidnapped her. Maisie froze. Was this to be her last moment? She started to pray silently for forgiveness for whatever she had done that had brought her to this place.

She heard the clatter of boots against metal and someone cursing quietly. The boy jumped over the bales of hay that were hiding Maisie, missing her leg as he landed, missing her by no more than an inch. He seemed older than Maisie had first thought when he had given her the cup of "water" and he was much dirtier. As he reached to cut the string around her ankles, he whispered, 'Don't you go getting any ideas about running or screaming or the like. If you do he will surely kill you. Make no bones about that!' Hauling her to her feet, he shoved her over the hay bales and towards the open doors of the wagon.

Peggy and Brian had enjoyed the time that they had spent together at the fair, Brian had won a doll for Peggy on the coconut shy and everything to the pair seemed just dandy. As they walked back towards the bench under the tree they were laughing and joking about the man on the coconut shy, who had seemed very surprised that someone had actually won. 'I don't think that he had rammed that coconut hard enough into the holder,' Brian had said as he had handed Peggy the little doll. Neither felt that they could be any happier and Peggy couldn't wait to tell her friend all about it. On seeing the empty bench under the tree, Peggy's heart almost stopped. Picking up her skirts, she started to run towards the now empty bench, shouting over her shoulder as Brian hurried to catch up with her. 'Brian, where is she? She promised not to move but to sit here and watch the carousel.'

'Don't panic, Peg, she's most probably already gone back to meet the others and wait for Jack,' he tried his best to soothe her.

'No, no. You don't understand, she promised. Maisie would never break a promise, especially to me.' Peggy kept circling the tree as if by doing this Maisie would suddenly appear.

'Come on now, Peg, let's not get ourselves in a stew.' He held his hand out to the distraught girl. 'Why don't we go back to the corner of the high street and see if she's there? I'll put my last penny on her being with the others.' Inside, he wasn't so sure. Something didn't feel right.

The two hurried through the fair, past the Red Lion pub and round the corner to the high street. A small group had gathered already waiting for Jack to pull the horse and cart round from the yard behind the pub. Peggy scoured the group but to her dismay, there was no sign of Maisie.

'Has anyone seen Maisie?' But the group was talking so loudly about their experiences at the fair that no-one heard her.

'FOR GOD'S SAKE, YOU LOT, SHUT UP!' The group immediately fell silent and stared, stunned, as they looked at Peggy, who was standing there with tears rolling down her face. 'Has anyone seen Maisie?' With that she crumpled to the floor in utter despair.

Brian explained to the other young servants what had happened as Bessie rushed forward to comfort Peggy. This was the scene that greeted Jack as he rounded the corner with the horse and cart. He had been expecting to see a group of very excitable youngsters but instead they were all standing looking as if someone had died. Tom walked around to the far side of the cart and relayed to his father what Brian had just told them.

Without hesitation Jack addressed the little crowd. 'Right then, listen to me.' He spoke from his seated position. 'Girls, go in pairs and stay in pairs and search every bit of the fair. You boys, again in pairs, search all of the surrounding streets. I'll go and check in the Red Lion and the White Hart. Go on, then. No time to waste. Be back here in half an hour.'

As they all returned, Jack was becoming more and more worried. He was sure that one pair would have come across Maisie but no such luck. Rubbing his hand through his hair, a habit he had when he was trying to work out a solution, he turned to his son. 'Right Tom you take the reins and get this lot back to the Park, I'll stay here and keep searching for her. Peggy, when you get back go straight to Cook and tell her what has happened. The rest of you, no dramatics. I'm sure that everything will be all right.'

'Brian can master the cart, Dad. I want to stay and help you, two pairs of eyes are better than one.' As he spoke, Tom gestured to Brian to get up in the driver's seat.

Jack didn't argue he knew that Tom had always had a bit of a soft spot for Maisie and looking at his son's worried face, he couldn't turn him away.

After the cart had left, Tom turned to his father. 'Should we let the bobbies know? The fair leaves town tonight and, well, if anything has happened to her—' his voice trailed away. He really didn't want to think about it.

Tom nodded his head and set off towards the police station. They spent about half an hour going over and over what they knew. No, she was not the type of girl to be "Found in some pub bedroom plying her trade", as the policeman had put it. No, she would not have just run away. Yes, she was happy living at the Park.

In the end, in utter despair Jack demanded that they help them to search for her. Reluctantly, the three policemen who were on duty agreed. They'd been hoping to slip in for a quiet beer. The landlord at the Red Lion was always very generous to the policemen and would let them into the back room from the stable yard, where no one could see them drinking.

Jack and Tom were told to keep searching the fair and the policemen would search the alleyways and stable yards. On entering one yard at the back of a scruffy row of houses, PC Doyle came across a large wagon being loaded with the pieces of a disassembled stall. A large man and a younger boy were busily loading it; they seemed agitated to see him there.

'Well, now, what are you two up to this fine afternoon?' PC Doyle put on his most commanding voice. 'What have you got in that wagon?'

'Oh, sir, we were just making sure that we have all of the parts of our stall,' the older man said in a pathetic tone. 'Nothing else, sir.'

'Why are you packing up so early? The fair doesn't finish until late tonight, surely you're missing some good trade?' the PC asked.

'The thing is, sir, my wife isn't at all well and I promised that I would be back tonight. You're right though, sir, it tears me up to miss the trade but what can I do?' He wrung his hands as if in pain.

PC Doyle peered into the back of the wagon. Sure enough, apart from a couple of bales of hay stacked at the back, nothing seemed out of place. 'All right, then, get going.' With that the PC walked out of the yard.

'Come on, we need to get this loaded.' The big man started to throw the rest of the pieces into the back of the wagon. 'Get in, we'd better get out of here whilst we still can, we don't want to be here if the bobbies come sniffing around again.'

Poor Peggy

Peggy thought that Cook was going to faint as she told her what had happened at the fair. Jennie quickly steered Cook towards the little table in the corner of the kitchen. 'Sit down and I'll make you a nice cup of tea.' Jennie darted a sympathetic look at Peggy who was standing, head bowed and tears streaming down her face. 'I think that you had better sit down as well, Peggy. Come on, dear, now settle yourself and tell us again what exactly happened.'

Peggy told them everything, starting from when they got there to when she left Maisie sitting on the bench near the tree.

'I told you both to stay together,' Cook whispered. 'How could you have left her on her own?'

Peggy immediately started to cry again.

'I'm sure that the door will open in a minute and Jack will march in and tell us all is well and that Maisie is safe.' Jennie didn't really believe this and she was unable to look either of them in the eye.

A loud knock on the back door made them all jump. Jennie hurried over and on opening it, saw that it was only Brian. Looking past him, in the distance there was Jack and Tom hurrying across the yard. On catching Jennie's eye Tom shook his head. 'Come in, come in, the three of you.' Jennie stood to one side and the three men walked slowly into the kitchen.

'Please tell me that you have found her,' Peggy pleaded.

'The bobbies have turned the town upside down and there's no sign of her.' Tom was close to tears. 'Peggy, please think. Did you see anyone hanging around when you left her?'

Peggy looked at Brian and he thought that his heart would break, she looked so pitiful. 'There was no-one near the seat when we walked away and she said – well, she promised Peggy – that she would not move from there, she just wanted to watch the carousel,' Brian answered for Peggy.

'Oh, dear lord!' Cook suddenly exclaimed. 'Someone will have to tell Mrs Dean and Mr Shore.' They all looked at Cook.

'Oh, dear lord, there is going to be trouble with a capital T. What on earth is the family and Miss Brockenhurst going to say, and as for Lady Elizabeth, she is going to be heartbroken.'

'What is going on?' came a very stern voice from the passageway. Mrs Dean entered the kitchen closely followed by Mr Shore. 'Well, speak up, someone. Why will Lady Elizabeth be heartbroken, what have you all been up to?'

Cook slowly stood up. 'I think that it will be better if we talk in your sitting room, if you don't mind, Mrs Dean.'

After a few minutes, the door to Mrs Dean's sitting room flew open. 'PEGGY, COME HERE NOW!' screamed Mrs Dean.

Peggy immediately jumped to her feet. 'She's going to send me away,' she whispered.

Brian grabbed her hand as she walked past him. 'Don't worry, love, I'm here,' he gently told her.

After what seemed liked hours, but was most probably only half an hour Mrs Dean and Mr Shore emerged from the sitting room and disappeared along the passageway towards the main house. They were followed by Cook and Peggy, who came back into the kitchen.

'They've gone to tell Lady Willaby,' Cook said quietly. 'They thought it best to tell her first, rather than Miss Brockenhurst. I think that they are hoping that by telling her she will come up with some sort of plan for telling Lord Willaby and Lady Elizabeth. Jennie, dear, would you mind making everyone a cup of tea, I think it is going to be a very long night.'

Although Peggy was sitting next to the fire she was shivering. Looking at Brian she said, 'They haven't decided what is to happen to me, but Mrs Dean said to expect the worst.' At this, tears started to well up in her already swollen eyes. 'If they put me out what am I to do? I have nowhere to go.' She put her head in her hands. 'How I wish that I had stayed with Maisie, whatever happens to me is my own fault, I shouldn't have left her.'

The kitchen clock struck midnight and as there was no sign of either Mrs Dean or Mr Shore, Cook told the little group that they should all retire to bed as nothing else could be done that night. The group all went their separate ways.

Brian looked at Peggy as he spoke to Cook. 'Can I come back in the morning to make sure that she's all right?'

Cook just nodded her head and taking Peggy's arm, led her out of the kitchen towards the back stairs that lead up to the servants' quarters.

After making sure that Peggy was safely in bed and hugging the little doll that Brian had won for her, Cook quietly went back down to the kitchen. As she passed the door to Mrs Dean's sitting room she heard muffled voices coming from within. Not stopping to knock, she entered to find Mr Shore and Mrs Dean sitting next to the fire, deep in conversation.

'Is there any news?' As she spoke, Mrs Dean beckoned her to join them. 'What did Lady Willaby say?'

'Both the master and mistress were in the drawing room.' Mrs Dean spoke quietly. 'Lord Willaby has said that he will send the farm workers into the town at first light to search again for Maisie.' At this she shook her head. Her voice dripping in sarcasm, she continued, 'Whoever would have thought that so much fuss would be made of a servant girl.'

'But she's no longer just a servant girl, she's Lady Elizabeth's companion and I don't care what anyone says,' with that, Cook shot Mrs Dean a sharp look, 'I know that Maisie would not have just disappeared of her own choosing, she adored Lady Elizabeth and was so happy living here.'

Mr Shore stood and stretched. 'I agree with you, Cook. Now, Margaret, don't look at me like that.' Mrs Dean sharply inhaled and narrowed her eyes at him. 'I know that you think she's just run off with some lad, but I don't. Now it is very late and I would suggest that we all get some sleep.' He started to walk towards the door. 'Oh, Cook, I nearly forgot. You can tell Peggy in the morning that her job is still safe and that no blame is being laid at her door.' With that, he bid the two women goodnight.

Lord Willaby was as good as his word: at break of day two wagons full of farm workers, one driven by Jack and the other by Tom, set off towards the town. Lord Willaby had handed Jack a handwritten note which was to be given to the police sergeant with strict instructions that his officers were to do everything possible in finding Maisie. On reading the note, the sergeant looked at Jack. 'What do you really think has happened, has she run off with the fair or some lad?'

'No, sir, I don't think she has. Something doesn't feel right. She wasn't the flighty sort and as far as I know, never had an admirer.' He looked down at his boots. 'I am worried that something dreadful has happened to her.'

'Right then, best get on with it. We can't have Lord Willaby's men standing around doing nothing.' The sergeant marched past Jack, through the outer office and when he reached the top of the steps leading into the police station he blew his whistle to get the men's attention.

'Okay now, I need you to split into groups. My men will be the leader of each group and if you find anything they will blow their whistles. No stone is to be left unturned.'

Immediately the workers and the policemen shuffled around until four equal groups had been organised. They all set off in different directions with the policemen in the lead.

Hours went by with no sound of a whistle. A lot of the town's men had also joined in the hunt and some of the women were busy scurrying around with jugs of water to quench the searchers' thirst.

'Aren't you going to help? After all, I thought that the girl that's gone missing is your granddaughter. Well, that's what everyone is saying,' one old lady said as she hurried past where Mrs Callow was sitting, enjoying the morning sun as if nothing extraordinary was happening.

'Huh, no way. They're all wasting their time.'

The old woman stopped and looked at Mrs Callow, who continued, 'Turned after her father, that one, no good from the start. Help search? She'll be miles away by now with some no-good lad. Help search? Not likely.'

The old woman could have sworn that she saw a brief smile cross the other woman's face.

'Well, perhaps you should tell that to the bobbies so as not to waste any more of everyone's time. Shall I call the sergeant over?' She opened her mouth as if she was about to shout.

'No, no. It's only my opinion. I don't know anything and I could be wrong.' As she spoke, Mrs Callow stood up and hurried away down the street towards her home.

The old lady stood for a moment looking after the retreating figure. 'Mmm, I think that maybe you do know something,' she muttered to herself.

The light was beginning to fade as the weary men all met back in the town square. The hope that they had felt in their hearts at the beginning of the day had faded with the light. Jack and Tom brought the wagons round and after thanking the policemen for their help, the weary group started back in silence towards the Park.

Mrs Durrant

'Daniel, for Christ's sake, what's taking you so long?' The man's angry voice made Maisie jump. 'For god's sake, we haven't got all bloody night.'

The boy hauled Maisie roughly to her feet and pushed her over the bales of hay towards the wagon doors. There she saw that the man was talking to an elderly lady who was dressed from head to toe in black. She was slightly hunched over and when she turned towards the back of the wagon Maisie's heart jumped; her face was pinched and badly scarred. She reminded Maisie of a picture of a witch that she had seen in one of Lady Elizabeth's story books.

The man stepped forward and grabbed Maisie's arm, pulling her roughly down to the ground. 'Well, Ma, do you think that you can use this one?' He hesitated as the old woman looked her over.

'Bit of a miss, ain't she? Looks like she's never done a day's work in her life in all them fine clothes.'

'I was told she's a servant from the big house,' he replied. 'Must admit I was taken by surprise when I saw her, but the old bag pointed her out as the one, so we must have got it right.'

'Is she wanted by the bobbies?' Without waiting for his reply she continued, 'Get her in the house before any of these nosey buggers see her.' She gestured at a row of small cottages on the opposite side of the road.

On her command, the man and the boy who had now been identified as Daniel frog marched the stunned girl into the house. On entering, the smell made Maisie want to gag. The sitting room cum kitchen was stale with the smells of cooking, smoke and another that Maisie couldn't identify.

'How much did she pay you?' the old woman was asking the big man.

'Half a crown, that's all, Ma. But I thought you always need help, so I took it.' He was looking at his shoes like a little boy.

'Half a bloody crown? What do you think I am, a bloody idiot?' With this she reached forward and gave him a hearty whack across the top of his head. 'Now tell me the truth or you'll get another.'

Maisie, even in the state that she was in, was amazed to see this big brute of a man acting like a child in front of this old woman.

'Ma, please don't hit me again. Here's the money and I promise, that's what she gave me.' With this he handed the woman some coins, which she immediately put in the pocket of her dirty dress.

'Right then.' Turning to where Maisie had been forced to stand, she continued, 'This is a sticky problem. How am I to use her without anyone being suspicious? What's your name?'

Maisie meekly replied and was about to say something else.

'Keep your mouth closed, I only asked for your name.' The spiteful reply was said over the woman's shoulder as she walked across the room and sat herself down in an old rocking chair next to the fire. 'Maisie, is it? Well, not any more, my girl.

From now on you will be Violet, my sister's girl from up north.' At this she gave a satisfied nod. 'You will not speak to anyone unless one of us is with you, if you do, well, God help you.

'Now then, Burt.' This was addressed to the big man. 'Get her a blanket from in there.' She pointed a gnarled finger at a cupboard in the corner of the room. 'You sleep in there, take that candle.'

Maisie looked to where the woman was pointing at the kitchen table., Bending to the fire she lit it and taking the blanket from Burt, she opened the door and entered what was to be her new bedroom.

The room was in complete darkness and she was glad that the woman had given her the candle, as the only other light came from the moonlight which streamed in through the small window near the ceiling. Maisie looked around the room, which was no bigger than a cupboard and saw that what laughingly passed as a mattress had been thrown on the floor. Although it was filthy, she wearily sat down and thought about what had happened in the space of the day. It had started off so happy, with the fair and seeing Peggy with her new beau; now it had ended like this. She went over in her mind the conversation that Burt and his mother had just had about being paid, when she was suddenly struck by a terrible thought. Shaking her head, she said to herself, 'No, she wouldn't pay someone to get rid of me. She's always after money, not one to spend it.' She convinced herself that in the morning Burt would tell her it had all been a terrible mistake and that they had taken the wrong girl. With that she drifted off into a fitful sleep.

Maisie jumped as the door to the room was thrown open. 'Get up, you lazy good for nothing.' The old woman's voice cut through Maisie like a knife. 'Put these on and get out here, double quick.' The woman threw an old brown dress on the floor and stomped away.

The smell of the dress made Maisie heave; it had a nasty, musty smell and was scratchy and horrible on her skin. She wanted to have a wash but thought better of asking, as washing didn't seem to be on the agenda for her this morning.

Walking out into the kitchen, she saw that other than the old woman the room was empty.

'Right, pin your lugholes back, cause I'm only telling you this once. Go out the back and bring in the logs, the fire's nearly out. Then get breakfast going. Those men will want a hearty meal before they go. When you've done that you can start cleaning in here.' She looked around the room. 'As you can see, I haven't been able to do it, so I want everything sparkling clean, just like that big house you're from.' With that the old woman chuckled, 'And if you need to speak to me, you will call me Mrs Durrant.' With a final nod of her head, 'Well, don't just stand there, get going.'

This was the first time that Maisie had been able to really see the inside of the house. Last night everything was in near darkness but now, looking around in the daylight, Maisie's heart sank. The house seemed to be just one main room downstairs, with a smaller room at the back. Everywhere she looked was covered in a thick layer of dust or dirt. The window facing the road was filthy, with rags that must be the poor excuse for curtains hanging limply at either side of the opening. The flagstone floor was caked in dirt and the smell in the room was overpowering. The only area that wasn't covered in dust was the big table at the centre of the room, but this had stains of dried spilt food all over it. Maisie couldn't understand how people lived like this. Even though she had hated living at her nana's, at least it was clean.

Maisie walked through the kitchen and into the little room at the back, which was even more smelly than the kitchen. The flagstone floor looked as though it had also never been cleaned and was smeared with grease, as was the old battered sink which ran along one side of the room. Other than a broken cupboard there was no other fixtures in there. Maisie opened the creaky back door and walked out into the fresh air. Inhaling deeply, she looked around. To one side of the courtyard was a log store and an outside water closet; mostly the small courtyard seemed to hold broken pieces of fairground stalls.

She was pulled back to reality by the sharp voice of the woman. 'Violet, what the hell is taking you so long?' For a moment Maisie didn't realise that it was her that the old woman was shouting at. 'Violet get yourself in here now.'

Maisie said to herself, 'Violet, I must remember that I am Violet.'

Shocking News

Maisie had been missing for six months when the police sergeant arrived at the Park. He was shown into the sitting room where Lord and Lady Willaby were waiting for him. After about an hour, the sergeant left. Chris Brown was summoned to the sitting room and was given instructions to ask Mr Shore and Mrs Dean to gather all of the servants together in the servants' hall.

'Well, what's it all about?' Cook looked at Mrs Dean. 'Have they found Maisie, is there news?'

Mrs Dean shrugged her shoulders. 'Honestly, I don't know, all Chris Brown said was that Lord Willaby wants everyone in the servants' hall. So come along, no more questions. He'll be down soon.'

Cook, Jennie, Peggy and Bessie all followed her in silence along the passageway and into the servants' hall, where Mr Shore and the rest of the house servants were waiting. After what seemed like hours Lord Willaby entered the room.

Standing at the front, he looked around and on seeing Peggy. he asked Chris Brown to please fetch chairs for her and Cook.

'I'm sure that most of you already know that Sergeant Murray came to see Lady Willaby and me this morning.' He stopped and cleared his throat. 'The news that he has brought is unfortunately not what we wanted to hear. A woman's body has been found at the top of Mount Pleasant, the group of hills which are approximately ten miles north of here.'

Peggy let out a scream and was immediately quietened by Cook, who also looked on the verge of fainting.

'I know that this is a shock for you all, as it was for Lady Willaby and myself, but as no other female has been reported missing in the area, the police have to assume that it is Maisie. Lady Willaby is at present breaking the sad news to Elizabeth and Miss Brockenhurst.' He paused. 'We have asked Sergeant Murray to be allowed Maisie's body for burial here at the Park and he has agreed that this should be possible.

'I think that I speak for everyone when I say that this is not the outcome that we had all hoped for.' Turning to where Mr Shore and Mrs Dean were standing, he continued, 'I'm sure that you will agree to relieve Peggy of all of her duties for the rest of the day,' and looking back to the two woman he added, 'Cook, would you be kind enough to make sure that Peggy is looked after. Peggy, I want to give you my absolute assurance and to inform everyone here that no blame is laid or should be laid at your door.' At that he nodded to the butler and housekeeper and made his exit.

Two weeks had passed when the news came that Maisie's body could be released and a date was set for the following week for the funeral. Jack felt that as he had driven Maisie to the Park on the first day, it would only be right for him to drive her on her last journey. He had approached Mr Shore, who had relayed his request to Lord Willaby, who had agreed that this would indeed be a fitting tribute.

In the days leading up to the funeral Jack and Tom had scrubbed and repainted the wagon until it looked like new. All of the horse brasses had been polished and on the day of the funeral Jack and Tom had got up extra early and had groomed Old Ned until his coat shone in the sunshine. Peggy and Bessie had collected flowers and leaves from the hedgerows and had made a lovely wreath, which was to be placed on Maisie's coffin and later, on her grave.

At 10.00 on the day of the funeral, Jack and Tom arrived at the undertaker's and carefully loaded Maisie's coffin onto the wagon.

'Rum old do, this,' said Mr Gray the undertaker. 'I don't suppose they will ever find out what exactly happened to her.'

Jack shook his head, thanked Mr Gray and with Tom by his side, steered the wagon along the narrow alley to the main street. The sight that greeted them surprised them both; the town's people had turned out in force and were lining both sides of the main street. Woman stood with their heads covered; some were crying and the men stood cap in hand as the wagon carrying the little coffin passed by. Jack could never remember this happening before; he had never seen the town or its people so quiet. One old lady approached the wagon as they passed and handed Tom a little sprig of white heather. 'Place this in her grave for me, it will bring her luck in the next world.' Tom nodded his thanks and the old lady took her place back at the side of the road.

The little estate church was full to capacity when they arrived, with people having to stand outside. Tom and Jack walked slowly to the back of the wagon and were joined by Brian and Chris Brown. As the church clock struck 12.00 noon the four men carried Maisie into the church.

That evening, Mrs Callow pulled on her best black hat. She had thought about giving the pub a miss tonight so that people would think that she was mourning the loss of her granddaughter but the pull of a pint of beer was too much for her. Looking at herself in the small cracked mirror near the door, she smiled she felt that now everyone thought that the girl was dead and buried, everything would go back to normal. Not once before today had she wondered what had really happened to Maisie; after paying the big fat bloke and the dopey boy to take her away she didn't really care what had happened to her, but she knew that the body that had been buried wasn't Maisie, she knew that for sure. The man had talked about taking her to Devon, but she wasn't overly bothered and hadn't really taken too much notice, just wanting the girl away from here. The incident at the Park still made her burn with anger, but now she felt that humiliation had been paid in full.

It was dark when she left the house and the rain was just starting to fall. Pulling her coat tightly around her, she headed towards the alley leading to the main road and the Red Lion pub. On entering the alley she was concentrating on picking her way over the cobbles when she became aware of someone standing in the middle of the walkway; it was a tall man, dressed completely in black, with the big black hood of his cloak pulled down over his face. In one hand he held a long wooden stick and with the other he grabbed her, throwing her against the wall, his hand clamped across her mouth.

'Now, you miserable old hag,' he growled. 'Where is she? I know that Maisie isn't dead and so do you. I want to know where she is.'

Mrs Callow shook her head and mumbled into his hand. 'The funeral was today; didn't you see it?'

'Don't treat me like a fool, I know that body wasn't Maisie.' A sudden noise at the other end of the alley startled the man. 'I'll be back and you had better have the answer for me.' With that he disappeared into the black of the night.

Mrs Callow stood for a long time against the wall, afraid to move in case he was around the corner. She abandoned the idea of the pub and hurried back to the relative safety of her home.

The Last Six Months

Every morning on waking, Maisie would tell herself that today was the day that the mistake would be discovered and she would be delivered back to her beloved home at the Park. She imagined the joy on Lady Elizabeth's face and the hugs and kisses she would get from her friends. But day after day she would retire to bed with a sinking heart.

Mrs Durrant was a very hard taskmaster and would work her from early morning into the night, scrubbing and cleaning. The filthy hovel that Maisie had first been brought into had been transformed into a clean and comfortable cottage, much to Mrs Durrant's delight.

On finding that Maisie was an exceptionally good cook and was an expert with a sewing needle, Mrs Durrant had formulated a plan. The first step had been to set up a little stall at the front door offering a range of pies and cakes, all, of course, made by Maisie. She was delighted at how well these sold and most nights Maisie would be cooking until well after midnight. She decided to let people get used to the pie stall and then she would start offering a tailoring service. She gave no thought to how poor Violet would manage to do everything, all she thought about was how much money she could charge people. These thoughts would keep her amused for hours as she sat in her old rocking chair next to the fire, sucking on an old clay pipe.

She was a shrewd old woman and knew that people wouldn't buy if both she and Violet looked dirty, so washing had become a priority, much to Maisie's delight. She had been allowed to alter her good dress to a more humble garment but at least it didn't scratch and tear at her skin like the old rag that she had first been given. However, this had given Mrs Durrant another idea. If the girl could alter and make clothes, why not offer this service as well? And so, on the back of Maisie's hard work, Mrs Durrant's empire had started to build.

On a bright, clear March morning Maisie had set the stall up at the front of the house as usual and Mrs Durrant had taken her seat next to it, ready for the first customer. Maisie had just walked back into the kitchen, hoping that now that the old woman was safely out of the way she might manage a quick cup of tea, when she heard, 'Violet, come here, dear.' Maisie hardly recognised Mrs Durrant's voice. 'Come along, dear, hurry up.'

She quickly walked towards the front door where she found Mrs Durrant in deep conversation with a man. He was tall and slim, with dark hair and he was wearing some sort of hat.

'Oh, there you are, dear,' Mrs Durrant cooed. 'Reverend Jones, this is my Violet.'

The man turned to Maisie and gave a little bow. 'I'm pleased to meet you, Violet. I was just expressing my compliments to Mrs Durrant on the wonderful cakes and pies that you make, they truly are quite delicious.' He couldn't believe that this wonderful-looking creature could possibly be related to the wizened old woman who presented her as her niece.

Maisie blushed. No one outside the house in the last six months had spoken directly to her. 'You are very kind, sir.'

Mrs Durrant watched this interaction and noticed the glint in the reverend's eye. Maisie was indeed very pretty and with the mannerisms that she had, she could be a lucrative catch for someone.

'I wonder, if I may be so bold, Mrs Durrant: sometimes I am given rabbits and ducks by kindly folk. My old housekeeper, Mrs Green, only ever makes stews or roasts and it would be nice to eat them some other way. Would it be possible for Violet to cook for me on occasion?' He paused and looked at the old woman and added, 'Of course, I would be willing to pay for her time.'

'I'm sure that Violet would be delighted, wouldn't you, dear?' She continued without waiting for Maisie to answer. 'Just let me know and I will arrange for Burt to drive her to the rectory, he can wait for her and bring her back when she's finished cooking.'

'No need for that, I'm always in the town. I can take Violet back with me and Burt can collect her after my meal.' Without waiting for a response from the old woman, he bid them both good day and walked off down the street.

The softness of the woman's voice vanished instantly when he was out of ear shot.

'Get inside and listen to me. Don't you go getting any ideas about blabbing to the nice reverend about your situation, 'cause no one, but no one, will believe you. Remember that you're a long way from home and hardly anyone knows you're here, so if you go missing again—' at that, her voice trailed off but from the look on her face Maisie knew that she would not say anything to anyone.

A couple of days later the reverend called at the house to ask if Mrs Durrant could spare Violet that afternoon, as he had been given a rabbit and would like her to cook it for him. Not wanting to make the man suspicious, Mrs Durrant had reluctantly agreed. This was the first time that the girl had been out of her sight and she felt very uneasy. By the time that the reverend pulled up at the door in his little pony and trap, Maisie's head was ringing from Mrs Durrant going on and on about what would happen to her should she open her mouth.

Maisie had packed a little basket of ingredients and some cooking implements, just in case, as Reverend Jones had stated that his housekeeper Mrs Green didn't really cook anything other than stews and roasts. On seeing Maisie, Reverend Jones jumped down from the trap and took the basket from her whilst helping her into her seat. He then stowed the basket carefully in the back of the cart and climbed up next to her, turning towards the house where Mrs Durrant was watching the scene nervously. 'No need to send Burt, Mrs Green's husband is coming into town this evening and will bring Violet home.' Before Mrs Durrant could object, he switched the reins and moved off.

The old woman stood on the doorstep glowering after them. Now someone else would have a chance to question the girl. As she turned to go inside a thought sprung into her head: 'Cheeky bugger, he hasn't even paid me!'

Maisie was astounded at the amount of attention their little journey was attracting. Men stopped as they saw them approach and raised their hats to the reverend, who casually waved in their direction, whilst the women's eyes darted from Maisie to the reverend and back again.

'Oh dear, I think that we are creating quite a stir,' the reverend chuckled. 'I bet my church will be fit to burst this Sunday.'

For the first time Maisie looked fully at the man sitting at her side. She thought that he was about thirty, with a kind but not handsome face. He was quite tall and angular and Maisie felt that he indeed needed feeding up. She liked the fact that he had a sense of humour and found the antics of the townsfolk amusing. The vicar who came to the little church at the Park had been a dry old stick, she could never imagine him laughing and chuckling.

On their journey, he pointed out various local beauty spots and places of interest to Maisie and was astounded that in the six months that she had lived with Mrs Durrant, she had not been to any of them. 'So tell me, Violet, other than cook and clean, what else do you do with your time?'

'I sew, sir. Some of the ladies can't afford to buy new so need their old dresses altered and as I can alter clothes Mrs Durrant says it would be wicked not to help others.' At this she looked down at her hands that were folded in her lap.

He started to laugh. 'No, Violet, you misunderstand me. I didn't mean what other work do you do, but what do you like to do with your free time?'

Maisie was hesitant as she was unsure how she should answer his question. Would he understand if she said that she had no free time, that Mrs Durrant worked her from morning to night to earn money for her keep?

'Well, when I can I like to draw, mostly flowers and landscapes, sir. I'm not really very good at drawing people.'

'Fantastic, I love to paint but I paint people and cannot for the life of me, however hard I try, make landscapes come to life. Maybe Mrs Durrant would allow you to come and paint in the rectory garden. I would love to have a painting of the garden in spring, it is so full of colour. With your permission I shall ask her. After all, Mrs Green is always around to act as a chaperone.' This last bit was more to himself than to Maisie. Maisie readily agreed that she would love to paint the garden but with a very heavy heart; she feared that Mrs Durrant would not allow it.

On arriving at the rectory, Reverend Jones walked Maisie through the house to the kitchen. It was quite small, with a cooking range on one side. A large wooden table ran down the centre of the room and on the end wall was a huge dresser with every type of cooking tin you could imagine. With so many, Maisie was surprised that Mrs Green didn't do much cooking. Sitting in the corner of the kitchen enjoying a nice cup of tea was an elderly couple, who looked up immediately when the newcomers entered the room.

'Oh, good, you are both here. I would like you to meet Violet. This is Mr and Mrs Green.'

The old man got to his feet. Holding out his hand, he walked across to shake Maisie's hand.

'I'm Ed and this is my wife Elsie. It's very nice to meet you.'

The lady stayed seated and out of politeness Maisie walked across to shake her hand.

'The tea's still hot in the pot, Joshua, if you and Violet would like a cuppa.' Elsie nodded towards the pot that was on the table.

Ed instinctively moved towards the table and producing two china cups and saucers from the cupboard at the side of the table, he started to pour out the tea. Handing a cup to both of them, he took his seat again opposite his wife.

'Well, Joshua here tells me you're a bit of a cook,' Elsie spoke directly to Maisie. 'So what delight are you going to conjure up for him today?'

Unsure if the woman was being sarcastic or not, Maisie tried to answer her question diplomatically. 'I expect it's strange for you to have someone else come into your kitchen, especially someone that you don't know, but I have tried to bring most things that I think I shall need. I thought maybe a rabbit pie, with some nice vegetables and thick beef gravy, followed by an apple pie. Fairly simple fare but usually quite tasty.'

Maisie noticed Ed lick his lips.

'I had one of your pies with a pint in the pub the other day and very tasty it was.' At this his wife shot him a dirty look and continued drinking her tea.

Looking at the clock Maisie addressed the reverend, who she now knew was Joshua. 'I think that I had better get started, if that's all right.' At this she looked at Elsie, who gave a little nod.

'Yes, yes, of course. Ed, I have told Mrs Durrant that you will take Violet back after we have eaten, I hope that's all right.' Ed agreed that it would be fine as he was taking Elsie to visit her friend and could drop Violet off on the way.

'Right, then, I shall leave you to your cooking. I have a sermon to write.'

'I'll be going, too; the weeding won't do itself.' Ed got up from his seat and pulling on his boots, made his way out to the garden, where he could be heard whistling as he walked down the garden path towards the shed at the bottom of the garden.

Maisie stood and looked at Elsie.

'Elsie, I hope you don't think that I'm intruding. When Mrs Durrant told me that I was going to cook for the reverend there was nothing I could do.' She looked so concerned that the older woman felt embarrassed at her earlier arrogance towards the girl.

'Don't you worry, dear. It's nice for me to be cooked for instead of doing it myself. We don't stand on the normal formalities here; we all eat together in the dining room.' She hesitated for a moment. 'I take it that you will be joining us, after all you have to wait for Ed and me. Now if there is anything you want me to do let me know, otherwise I shall sit here with my knitting.' With that she bent down and brought up what looked like a part finished jumper.

And so the weekly routine started. Maisie would be collected either by Reverend Jones, who she now called Joshua when at the rectory, or by Ed. Every single time Mrs Durrant would give her the same lecture until finally one day Maisie snapped. She couldn't take it anymore.

'Look don't you think that if I was going to say something I would have by now, for goodness sake? I don't see you saying NO to the silver shilling that you get every time I go to cook.' She wouldn't have got a better reaction if she had slapped the old woman in the face.

'I cook and clean all day for you and then you expect me to sit up all night altering clothes. Even servants get paid and have some time off, you know.' She gulped in some air and continued. 'Reverend Jones has asked me to paint a picture of the rectory garden and I don't care what you say, I'm going to do it and no, you are not going to get paid for my time.' On this she turned away from the now stunned woman and continued to pack her little basket. 'And before you hatch another plan, no. I am not going to paint pictures for you to sell, this is a one-off.'

The older woman sat in silence. She had never seen the girl like this, she had always been so compliant. Had she pushed her too far? she was a money spinner, there was no doubt about that. Churning it over in her head she decided that the girl was right; she had had ample opportunity to speak out or even run away and she hadn't, so a bit of free time wouldn't hurt. It might even make her work harder.

The Garden

About a month after the interaction with Mrs Durrant, Maisie sat in the rectory garden the paints and canvasses that Joshua had bought for her were neatly placed on the little wooden table next to her easel. So engrossed in her work was she that she didn't hear Joshua approaching. He stopped a few feet away and watched her paint fine, delicate strokes of paint that suddenly took life as different varieties of flowers on the canvas.

The garden was beautiful at this time of the year, with roses, both shrub and climbing varieties, the wonderful buddleia and the delicious smell of the honeysuckle that crept up the wall at the side of the lawn. With every slight movement the heady scent would fill the air.

This girl had made such a difference to his life that when she wasn't around, the old house felt quite empty. She filled his waking thoughts and now he found her intruding on his night-time dreams. He was so unsure of what to do as there was no father to approach about the prospect of having an official courtship and he didn't really feel that talking to Mrs Durrant was the answer; she would just want more money.

'Oh, hello. I didn't know you were there.' Maisie's voice brought him out of his daydream. 'You looked far away, is something troubling you?'

'I was just thinking about my sermon,' he lied. 'How's the painting coming on?' As he spoke he walked across the lawn and sat on the newly-mown grass beside her.

Turning to face him, she smiled. 'Fine, but I wish that the beautiful blue butterfly that was here earlier would come back, I'm ready to paint him now.' She laughed as she spoke; whenever she was here she could forget the pain of her past and the horror of living with the Durrants. 'What is your sermon about?'

'Well, that's the problem. I don't know. I have covered most every subject and am now running out of things that do not just cover exerts from the Bible. I like to have some happiness in my church, people have so many hardships in their lives that one thing that is free is humour.' He plucked at the grass near his leg.

She thought for a moment and then looking into his eyes she gently spoke. 'I think that you have your sermon, hardship versus humour. Oh, look, the blue butterfly! Joshua, you'll have to excuse me, but I need to paint him.' She moved back in front of her easel and taking up a slim brush started to paint.

Slowly, so as not to frighten the butterfly, Joshua stood up and brushed the grass from his trousers. Taking one final look at her painting, he made his way back into the house, mulling over the idea that she had given to him about his sermon.

On reaching his study he poured a small glass of brandy and settled himself at the desk that sat beside the door, which opened out directly into the garden. However hard he tried to concentrate on his writing, he found that his eyes kept wandering to where she was sitting. The slight breeze played with the strands of hair that had escaped from the bun at the base of her neck and her long dress moved slightly around her ankles. Shaking his head, he bent over the paper and started once again to write.

As the sunlight began to fade Maisie packed up her easel and paints and walked back towards the house. On seeing Joshua hunched over the desk, she headed for the open door of his study.

'How's the sermon going?'

'Your idea was brilliant and I've nearly finished it. Would you like me to read it to you?' He gestured for her to sit and started reading in what Maisie affectionately called his vicar's voice.

Elsie Green came hurrying down the garden. 'That brute's here,' she said to her husband, who was busy turning soil in the vegetable patch. 'He says that Violet has to go with him now, but she's in the study with Joshua and I don't want to disturb them. What shall I do?'

'Nothing for it, my dear. Go and get her, he'll only start trouble if you don't,' came the reply as he carried on with his work. He knew that his wife was troubled about the situation at Mrs Durrant's but Violet never talked about it and if pressed, she would quickly change the subject.

Mrs Green sighed as she tentatively knocked on the study door and informed Maisie that she was needed. On hearing that Burt was waiting for her Maisie excused herself and dutifully collected her things. Bidding Joshua and Mrs Green goodbye she slowly walked out to the wagon where Burt and Daniel were waiting for her.

''Bout bloody time,' was the greeting. 'Get in. Ma wants you to do some sewing in a hurry, the woman wants it back first thing in the morning.'

Maisie climbed up into the wagon. 'Oh well, back to reality,' she thought to herself.

The Painting

Over the past ten months Maisie had settled into a routine of once a week going to cook for Joshua at the rectory and then on her one day off a month, which was normally only half a day as Mrs Durrant always found something for her to do before she could go, she would go either to the rectory and paint or, as happened last month, Joshua would take her and Mrs Green, who always acted as chaperone, to a local beauty spot where Maisie would paint the landscape or flowers. Joshua had asked Maisie's permission to sketch her, although he said she couldn't see his work until he was completely happy with it. Mrs Green would either do her knitting or as often happened, fall asleep, snoring loudly. This would make Maisie giggle and she would mercilessly tease Elsie when she woke up.

The morning was bright and sunny when Maisie woke. She dragged herself out of bed and then suddenly remembered that today was her day off. Stretching, she thought, 'Right then, my girl, let's see what she's found for me to do today.'

To her surprise the kitchen was completely empty, but in the distance she could hear the sound of low voices. Unsure of where they were coming from, she started to walk towards the front door. She entered the hallway just in time to see Mrs Durrant closing the door.

'Well, that's buggered your day off.' The woman was unable to keep the smile from her face. 'That was Ed Green, he said the reverend has received a message that a vicar who is in the area would like to call on him today, so he doesn't think it fitting to have you there.'

Maisie stood in silence mulling over in her head the news and what it meant. What did he mean, not fitting? She wasn't doing anything wrong in being at the rectory, was she? The question spun round and round in her mind.

She was suddenly aware that the old woman was talking to her. 'Cloth ears, did you hear me?' The shout rang through the empty hallway. 'Get yourself in here, if you're not going out you can get on with this sewing Doris Brown brought it round late last night.' With that she threw a large pile of clothes on to the kitchen table. 'And when you've finished with that you can make a start on the rabbit pies, it's market day tomorrow so we should be able to sell a lot. Now stop day dreaming and get on with it.'

Maisie sat at the table and felt that her heart was breaking. 'Was Joshua so ashamed of her that he didn't want any of his friends to see her? She couldn't believe that he could be so heartless. Without a word, she picked up the first item of clothing and started to darn a hole in the knee. She stayed sitting at the table in silence for most of the day, only stopping to make the old woman cups of tea or something to eat. The day seemed to drag and with a very heavy heart, she was glad when it was time for her to retire.

Joshua was shocked to receive the message from Reverend Bird to say that as he was passing through Devon, he would very much like to stop by the rectory and meet with his dear friend Joshua and perhaps partake in a little lunch. Knowing that Robert Bird had a bit of an eye for the ladies, Joshua thought it prudent to change the day for Violet to visit. After all, Robert was a very handsome fellow and he didn't want Violet's head to be turned.

On finding Ed and Elsie in the kitchen, he asked Ed to go to Mrs Durrant's and enquire if Violet could come the next day and then turned to Elsie. 'Can you rustle up something for lunch? I'm sorry it's such short notice.'

'Well, we still have a couple of chicken pies from the last batch that Violet cooked and if I'm not mistaken – oh, yes, here it is—' she was rummaging through the pantry as she spoke. 'A lovely apple pie. I could make some custard to go with that.' She came back into the kitchen. 'I'll get Ed to bring in some vegetables. Don't you worry, lunch will be fit for a king.'

Joshua smiled his thanks and walked slowly back through the hallway to his study. He was gravely disappointed that he would not be seeing Violet today, he had so been looking forward to it. The painting that he had been slaving over was finally finished and he couldn't wait to show her, even though he said so himself it truly was a remarkable likeness. He had chosen the spot where it would hang, which was on the wall at the other side of the room facing his desk, so that whenever he felt down or lonely he would be able to see her.

The doorbell jolted him back to reality and he heard Elsie give her normal greeting. 'Good morning, sir. Reverend Jones is in his study.' The door opened and there was Robert Bird, as splendid as ever.

'Robert, dear fellow, how very nice to see you, what a surprise.' Joshua gave his friend a hug. 'Elsie, refreshments, if you'd be so kind.' Joshua smiled at his housekeeper and turned back to his friend. 'Well, what brings you to deepest, darkest Devon?'

'I'm on my way to Cornwall, I've been offered the bishop's position and wanted to go and look around before accepting.' Robert puffed out his chest with pride.

'My, my, a bishop! Well, if I'd known, instead of a hug I would have bowed in the presence of such an important person.' As he spoke he gave an elaborate bow. 'Now, come and sit down and tell me all of the news from Somerset, nothing exciting ever happens here.'

With that the two friends started to exchange titbits of gossip about their dioceses and other clergymen. Robert had a juicy bit about a vicar who had been found with someone else's wife and the scandal had proved too much for the man, who the week after had been found hanging from a tree. 'Ah, but the most surprising thing that happened is a young servant girl from one of the big houses went missing. Everyone assumed that she had run off with the fair that was visiting the town at the time, but then a body was found in the hills not far away.' He stopped and sipped his tea. 'I met her once. Very pretty little thing she was.'

After they had enjoyed their luncheon the two men went out into the garden.

'Don't you get bored in this backwater?' Robert enquired of his friend. 'I can't imagine living here with just the birds as company.'

'I fancy that you would prefer a different kind of company,' his friend teased. 'I suppose I've just got used to it. When I have to venture to the big city it seems so noisy and dirty that I'm always glad to get back.'

'My dear boy, you are going to end up a wizened old bachelor if you don't find yourself a wife soon.' His friend looked at Joshua with concern. 'How old are you now? Thirty? Thirty-five?'

'And what about you? I don't see any wife with you.' Catching a glint in his friend's eye, 'Oh, or is there something else you need to tell me?'

'You'll be the first to know if I decide that she's the one. Now can we go inside? It's starting to get chilly and I'm ready to sample some of that fine brandy that you normally have hidden away.' He slapped Joshua on the shoulder and they both walked, laughing, back into the house.

Whilst Joshua went in search of glasses, Robert looked around the study. Spying the easel with a cover over it he walked across and just as he had uncovered the painting, his friend walked back into the room. 'No, stop,' Joshua shouted but it was too late, Robert was already studying the picture.

'Who is this?' he questioned without taking his eyes off the lovely face that smiled out from the painting. 'Joshua, WHO is this?'

Joshua was startled at the reaction from his friend.

'That is Violet and I wanted her to be the first to see it. Why are you looking at me in that way? I have not taken advantage of this lovely girl, if that is what you think. Whenever I see her, Elsie always, but always, chaperones her.' He stopped talking and stared at his friend, who was studying the picture in great detail.

'Are you telling me that this girl lives in the town?' Turning to look at Joshua he continued, 'What do you know about her?'

'More to the point, what do you know about her?' came the reply

'Look, I may be mistaken but I'm sure that I have met this girl before.' He hesitated, not sure whether to share his thoughts with Joshua. 'Just, please, tell me what you know and that may sort out the jumble in my head.'

After listening intently to the story that Joshua told him, Robert gulped down the last of his brandy. 'I think that you had better get us both another, I think that you will need it.' After getting his friend to promise not to act on what he was about to say until after he had a chance to check everything out, he relayed the events that led up to Maisie's disappearance.

'Oh, dear lord. If that is true, we must ensure that she is set free. Both Ed and Elsie have mentioned to me that they felt something wasn't right and I myself have felt very uneasy about the situation at Mrs Durrant's. What should I do? I can't just barge in there and demand to know the truth.' Joshua shook his head in complete confusion.

'Please, Joshua, don't do anything. Not a word to the Greens. I will be back in Somerset at the end of the week. Let me do a bit of digging before you go blasting everything to kingdom come.' With this, he patted the man's leg. He could see that the situation deeply troubled him. 'Now promise me, dear friend. If you go in there demanding to know, you could do more harm than good. If they have spirited her away once, they could do it again, so no heroics. Do you understand?'

Joshua nodded his head. 'But it's going to be difficult. Please let me know as soon as you can.'

Later that afternoon, Robert got his driver to go very slowly through the town. There outside a house was a little pie stall, just as Joshua had told him.

'Driver, pull over.'

As the carriage stopped Robert stepped out and crossed the street. The old lady looked up and smiled at the handsome stranger standing in front of her.

'Did you make these fine-looking pies, madam?' he enquired.

For a split second she thought about lying, but decided that such a fine young gentleman might part more easily with his money on seeing Maisie.

'No, sir, my Violet made these. She's a very fine cook.' Without hesitating, and using her very best voice, she called for Violet to come to the front door.

Robert held his breath as from the darkness of the hallway, the young girl who he had seen before approached the doorway. She looked tired and thinner than he remembered but it was definitely and without question the same girl. 'I have been told by Reverend Jones that you make the best pies in Devon, so as I was passing I thought that I would buy some to take back to Somerset.'

At the mention of Somerset, the girl's eyes widened and she gulped in air, as if the very mention of the county had shocked her. 'Have you ever been to Somerset, my dear?' he continued but before she could answer, the old lady turned her around and sent her back into the house.

'Enough chitter chatter. The girl has work to do. Now, are you buying or not?' the old woman straightened up to her full height and looked him straight in the eye. 'If not, I'll bid you good day, sir.'

'No, I think that I'll leave it,' and with that he turned and walked back to his carriage. The old woman watched until they disappeared over the horizon, the meeting troubled her greatly.

As soon as Maisie had served up Burt and Daniel's meal the old woman had sent her to her room with the words ringing in her ears. 'Don't you come out until you're called.'

Maisie sat on the mattress on the floor with a sinking feeling in her stomach. Ever since the man from Somerset had called, Mrs Durrant had been acting funny and now coming from the room was raised voices.

'I don't know, but I'm sure he recognised her,' Mrs Durrant's shrill voice could be heard shouting. 'Why else would he have gone on about bloody Somerset, asking if she'd ever been there?'

Burt replied but Maisie couldn't hear what had been said, when Daniel suddenly blurted out, 'What if the bobbies find her here? We'll all be had up for kidnapping.'

'Shut your bloody mouth,' was the angry response from Burt, 'or I'll hit you from here to kingdom come.'

'No, just hang on, Burt. The boy's right, if she is found here we could all end up in jail and at my age, I don't want that.' She heard the scrape of chairs and then silence.

It was very early next morning when Maisie was roughly shaken awake. 'Come on, get up. You're going on a journey with Burt.'

Maisie clambered up from the mattress and ran after the old woman. 'Where is he taking me?' She suddenly felt very afraid. 'Will I be coming back?'

'No, get your things, you're going now.' The old woman spoke without looking at her.

'Please, can I say goodbye to Reverend Jones and the Greens? They have been so good to me.' A tear escaped from her eye and ran slowly down her cheek.

'Don't you worry, I'll explain to them.' The old woman rubbed her cheek, wondering how on earth she would explain it. 'Now get out there, Burt's waiting to go.'

Realising that there was no point in arguing, she picked up her small basket of belongings and made her way towards the front door.

'Mrs Durrant—' But before she could say anything else, the door to the kitchen was slammed shut.

At 10.00 Daniel brought the small cart around to the front of the house and Mrs Durrant, wearing her Sunday best, clambered awkwardly up onto the seat.

'What you going to tell them, Nan?' the boy asked as he flicked the reins for the pony to go. When she didn't answer, he continued, 'The reverend's an educated man. He won't believe any old claptrap and he was sweet on Violet. He's not just going to let this go—' Before he could add anything else he received an almighty thump across his head. The rest of the short journey to the rectory was in silence.

Mrs Green brushed down her dress as she rushed to answer the door. She was unable to hide her surprise at seeing Mrs Durrant standing on the doorstep.

'Can I help you? Violet isn't here.'

'I want to see the reverend,' came the curt reply. 'Now go and get him.'

'Well, how rude.' Elsie felt quite indignant at being spoken to in that manner and especially by this woman. 'He normally only sees people by appointment at this hour of the morning.' Mrs Green eyed the old woman; something about her demeanour struck Elsie as odd. It wasn't just her appearance, which in itself was strange, but something that the housekeeper couldn't put her finger on.

The old woman narrowed her eyes. 'He'll see me, tell him it's about Violet. Now hurry up, I haven't got all day.'

On hearing that the Durrant woman was at his door, Reverend Jones hurried through the house and escorted the old woman into his study.

'Beautiful painting.' She walked across to the still-uncovered easel. 'What a shame, such a beautiful face but such a wicked person.' She turned to face the startled man.

'Ran away, she has. Stole all my money and the little bit of silver that I had. Got up this morning and she's gone, after everything that I did for her, not even a goodbye.' With this she sniffed and held a handkerchief to her face as if she was about to cry. 'Worse still, after you had made her so welcome, not even a goodbye to you.'

'I can't believe that she has gone of her own free will.' He slumped into the nearest chair. Would he really never see her again? 'Are you sure that Burt hasn't taken her somewhere? I don't believe that Violet would steal from you.'

The woman straightened up and spat out, 'Are you saying that my Burt is a thief and a kidnapper? You should be careful about spreading rumours like that, and you being a man of God. I've said my piece so I'll bid you good day.' With that she stalked out of the room and slammed the front door after her. The meeting had not gone the way that she had wanted; her intention was to ask the reverend for some financial help. After all, it was only his word that no hanky panky had taken place with the girl. But that could wait for another day, she needed to think that through before she accused him. After all, she knew that it wasn't true so a plausible story would need to be presented. Yes, for now she would bide her time.

After the old woman had left Joshua sat with his head in his hands. He couldn't believe that Violet was a thief. After all, Robert had said that she was highly regarded member of staff at a big house and that they were devastated at her "death". No, he shook his head. It could not be true, but where had she gone? Or, more importantly, where had they taken her? He decided that Robert needed to know the new turn of events and he immediately started to track him down.

Mrs Callow had just settled down to enjoy her evening meal and was daydreaming about whether to have a pint or if she could afford a nice warming brandy at the Red Lion later that night, when a loud knocking on her back door brought her back to the present. 'Oh, who the hell is that now?' she muttered as she walked over to open the door. She had only managed to open it a crack when it was forced out of her hand and with a clatter, hit the stone wall of the kitchen. There, standing right in front of her, was her worst nightmare.

The man shoved her back into the house and dragged her through to the small sitting room at the front of the house, roughly pushing her into the old chair that she had just vacated. He stood over her. All she could see was a pair of piercing blue eyes staring out from the darkness of the huge black hood. She shuddered at the silence as he stood there just waiting without uttering a word.

'Who the hell are you? What business do you have, asking questions about my granddaughter?' When no reply was forthcoming and all of her bravado had been used, she didn't know what else to do but to tell him the truth. He obviously wasn't going to leave until she did.

'Look all right, all right. I'll tell you what I know. They said that for 1 Guineas they could take her away and all I know is that they were talking of taking her to Devon, some place called Puddle Bridge. Bloody silly name for a town, if you ask me.'

The man stayed silent.

'Honestly, that's all I know. Haven't heard a word about her since and glad of it I am.'

Without a word, he turned to go but as he did so, he made a sweeping movement across the old woman's throat and after that there was no more noise in the house.

Days later, a small group of women stood in the road as the two policemen forced open the front door of the small terraced cottage. The cottage was in complete darkness and one of the officers silently cursed as he banged his shin on the sharp corner of a table as he reached across to open the curtains. As he turned back to look at the room his colleague let out a, 'Bloody hell!'

On the table sat a congealed plate of food and sitting in the old chair next to the table, slumped to one side was the body of Mrs Callow. Her throat had been cut and from the looks of her she had been there for a few days. The younger officer, PC Hardwill, gagged; this was only his second week in the job and this was the first dead body he'd seen.

'Pull yourself together, lad,' was the stern rebuff from PC Doyle. 'You take upstairs and I'll look around down here. See if it looks like anything's missing.'

The young PC ran up the stairs, glad to get away from the gruesome sight in the sitting room. But it took him no more than a couple of minutes to look around. Upstairs there was only one small room, which contained a bed and a set of drawers. Nothing was amiss. Walking back down the stairs, he looked through to the small kitchen to see PC Doyle examining a wall. He quickly hurried past the body and joined his colleague in the kitchen.

'What is it?'

'It looks as though the door was opened with some force.' He indicated to the missing piece of wood in the door. 'And here,' he pointed to the wall, 'looks as though something has struck the wall recently.' Standing, he brushed dust from his trousers.

'What do you think happened? It doesn't look as though it was a burglary.' The young officer scratched his head as he looked around the scruffy little kitchen.

'Don't expect she had anything to steal anyway, this is hardly the Ritz.' PC Doyle walked back into the sitting room and taking a cover from the chair next to the unlit fire, he covered the woman's body. 'Well, we had better go and put that lot out of their misery.' He inclined his head towards the front door, knowing that the women wouldn't have moved a muscle in case they missed something juicy.

On leaving the house, he said quietly, more to himself than to his young colleague, 'I don't think many will shed a tear.' PC Hardwill just nodded and the two walked silently out into the bright sunshine. After informing the group of women they slowly walked back to the police station to report what had been found.

The following week the man finally arrived at the edge of Puddle Bridge. It didn't look a very big place and so as not to cause any suspicion, he decided to camp in the hills surrounding the town and would venture down after dark.

As darkness fell an old wagon made its way along the main street and turning into an alleyway, disappeared from view. The man had been sitting watching for most of the day and other than normal everyday activities, nothing unusual had caught his eye. He made his way silently through the labyrinth of small alleys, trying as much as possible to avoid the main streets.

Every now and again he would stop outside a cottage window and listen to the conversations which were going on between various family members, but there was no mention of the girl.

As he passed by the church, he quickly ducked down behind a gravestone as he realised that someone else was in the graveyard. Two people, an older man and what looked like a vicar, were standing just outside the main church doorway., He tried as hard as he could to hear the conversation but they were talking very quietly and he was unable to hear much. He thought that he heard the names Violet and Durrant but was unsure; they certainly weren't talking about Maisie.

The days passed slowly as he watched over the town from his hiding place, hoping that one day he would see her. Night after night he ventured into the town, searching and listening to quiet conversation, until one night as he passed by a very run-down cottage he heard shouting from inside. 'Burt Durrant, don't you have that attitude with me. My sister doesn't want her there any more so go and get her.' The name Durrant made the man stop; that was the name that he had heard in the graveyard. He crouched down under the window and listened.

'But you told everyone that she's a thief, so if I bring her back no one will want to deal with you or her again. Why don't I just get rid of her? Save us all a lot of trouble,' a man's deep voice answered.

'No, I don't want her dead. Well, not yet. But you're right, we can't bring her back here. Who else do we know that would take her?' The conversation stopped and the man slipped away into the night, wondering who they had been talking about.

Later, sitting next to his camp fire he started to mull over what he had heard: didn't want her dead and couldn't bring her back to the town. Had someone rumbled them and they were the ones who had taken Maisie? He looked into the fire, maybe things were becoming clearer.

The New Place

It was now six weeks since Maisie had been moved to this new place. It turned out it was Mrs Durrant's sister's smallholding in deepest Cornwall. The journey had been horrific, as the roads where no more than lanes with grass growing up the middle and Burt had not been in the best of moods, swinging the wagon from one side to the other and cursing out loud.

Finally, they turned a sharp corner and there stood a large house surrounded by woodland. A cow stood looking at them over a nearby gate whilst chewing a mouthful of grass and she could see a couple of horses in a paddock next to the house. There were chickens and geese roaming freely and somewhere she could hear a dog barking in the distance.

As Burt brought the wagon to a stop the door of the house shot open and there, standing on the old rickety porch, was Mrs Durrant's sister. She looked nothing like her sister; this lady was small and round, with white hair pulled neatly back in a bun. Her clothes were clean and she had on a lovely flowery apron; she looked as though she had been baking. Burt jumped down from the wagon and walked over to her. After speaking for a few minutes the woman gestured to Maisie and the girl approached the house.

'Well now, my dear, I understand that you will be staying with me for a while.' She smiled at Maisie. 'I'm not a wealthy woman, so I'm afraid you will have to earn your keep.' With this she turned and they all entered the house. Closing the door quietly, Maisie looked around and was pleasantly surprised to see a clean, although shabby, sitting room that led straight through to a kitchen.

'Come through, dear, don't just stand there. Right, now, Burt, I know that you won't say no to a bit of breakfast. What on earth was the time, the two of you set off?'

'Don't know but it was early, you know what Ma is like when she gets a bee in her bonnet,' he said as he grabbed for a thick slice of bread.

'I am Mrs Campbell, but you can call me Joyce.' The woman stood looking at Maisie. 'And what do we call you?'

Both Maisie and Burt answered at the same time.

'Maisie.'

'Violet.'

'Maisie Violet.' Mrs Campbell shook her head. 'That's a bit of a mouthful, so what's it to be, Maisie or Violet?'

'Maisie, my name is Maisie.' She shot a dark look at Burt, who was chewing very noisily on his bread.

'Good, well now, Maisie, is that all of your belongings?' She indicated the small basket that the girl was holding. When Maisie nodded the woman tutted. 'Well, my sister is a bit of a skinflint, I'll see what I can find.'

After Burt had eaten his fill he bid his aunt goodbye and turning the wagon around, set off for Puddle Bridge. As Maisie watched him go a wave of relief suddenly hit her and she felt as if she was about to faint. Clutching at the post of the old porch, she gulped in deep lungful of clean country air.

The woman watched and although her sister had warned her not to ask any questions, she couldn't help but wonder how on earth this lovely creature had ended up lodging at her disgusting sister's home.

'Come along, dear, you look completely done in.' The old woman put an arm around Maisie's shoulders and steered her back into the house. 'Now, I think a wash and a nice sleep will do you the world of good.'

Maisie looked at the kind woman with tears in her eyes. 'Why are you being so kind to me?'

The woman gave a little laugh and patting her hand, she said, 'Because I think that you need someone to look after you. Now come along and I'll show you your room.'

By the time that Maisie woke it was late afternoon, looking around the little room she saw that the woman had put a dress on the chair next to her bed. It was lovely, if a little worn and slightly too big for Maisie's slender frame but she didn't care; at least it was clean. She tried to tidy her hair but found it impossible to get a bun to stay in place, so a ponytail would have to do for today.

Silently she crept out onto the little landing and was about to descend the stairs when she heard angry voices coming from the direction of the kitchen.

'What the hell has your sister got you into now?' a man's angry voice shouted. 'Some waif and stray and you just let them bring her here without knowing anything about her? She could be a murderer for all you know, we could all have our throats cut by morning.'

'You're wrong, Jed, wait until you meet her. She's a frightened little thing. Goodness only knows what they have done to her.' Joyce spoke gently to the man. 'My sister says she's a very good cook and seamstress and I could use some help around here, and it's not for long.'

'Well, on your head be it, but the first sign of trouble and out she goes.' With that, Maisie heard a door slam.

On entering the kitchen, she found Joyce sitting at the table, looking into her tea cup.

'I couldn't but help hearing.' Maisie looked towards the back door. 'I promise that I'm not a murderer and I won't slit anyone's throat.' Seeing the amusement in the older woman's eyes, she continued with a smile. 'But I am a good cook and not afraid of hard work.'

'He's just letting off steam, thinks that I should have asked him first.' The woman gestured for Maisie to sit and pushing a cup towards her, started to pour tea from a large brown earthenware teapot. 'My son thinks that he runs the place and is the man of the house, even though he lives down in the town with his wife and children and is of no help to me here.'

'I'm not sure where I am, all Burt would tell me was somewhere in Cornwall.' Maisie wasn't sure if she should be asking, but for her peace of mind, it would be nice to know.

'We're on the edge of Bodmin Moor, my dear.' With that the woman stood. 'This won't get the work done. Come with me and I'll show you what needs to be done.'

Walking out into the late afternoon sunlight, Maisie suddenly felt at peace. After months of every waking moment being filled with fear, she suddenly felt that maybe here, she could be herself.

Over the coming weeks, Joyce taught Maisie how to milk the old cow and how to groom and fasten the horses to the little carriage that they used to go into the town to collect essential supplies. With all the fresh air and the good wholesome food, Maisie started to lose the gaunt, drawn look that she had arrived with and as she filled out, Joyce marvelled at the girl's unusual beauty.

She had first noticed the impact that Maisie had on the opposite sex the first time she took Maisie into the town. The men made way for them on the walkways and doffed their caps whilst wishing them good morning. Doors were held open. They always seemed to be served first in the little café off of the high street; when Joyce had gone there on her own it was as if she was invisible and would sit for an age before being served, but now chairs would be held for them to sit and often they would be brought a complimentary slice of something delicious to enjoy with their morning coffee. She smiled to herself. Having the girl around brought its rewards.

During the six weeks since Maisie had arrived at Pond Farm, Jed had finally accepted that she wasn't a murderer and wasn't about to slit anyone's throat. In fact, when they were all together they would tease him about it.

Jed owned a greengrocer's shop in the main street of Bodmin Vale, along with his wife Prudence, who everyone called Pru. She was a pleasant little thing, extremely slim, with a mop of bright ginger hair and very pale skin. They had two very healthy-looking sons, Dick and Dan, who, whenever they visited Pond Farm would disappear for hours, making dens in the wooded area behind the house.

Joyce and Maisie were busy in the kitchen as the little family arrived, the smell of cooking making Jed's mouth water. As he entered the kitchen, he was laughing at something his wife had said.

'What are you two up to?' his mother questioned without looking up from her sewing.

'I said, you go on ahead and leave me to sort out the children. His eyes are bigger than his belly, he's just polished off a huge breakfast.' Pru eyed her husband's protruding stomach, patting it as she sat down opposite her mother-in-law.

'It's not my fault, it's hers.' He pointed at Maisie, who stuck her tongue out at him; this made the other two women laugh. 'If she didn't cook such delicious pies, I wouldn't have this.' He stroked his stomach and gave a very satisfied smile.

'Force feed you, do I? Hold you down and push the food down your throat?' At this the kitchen erupted with laughter. Maisie didn't think that she could be any happier than at that precise moment.

'I didn't expect to see you today, thought you were off to Padstow with the boys.' Joyce looked at her son who immediately looked at this wife.

'Well, go on then, you big lump,' Pru teased her husband. 'She's not going to bite.'

Sitting down, he mumbled, 'Thought I might have a cup of tea first,' looking hungrily at the freshly baked scones that were cooling on the wire tray on the table, 'and something to go with it.' When no one moved to oblige and with all eyes on him, he continued. 'Pru and I were talking. We have a section at the back of the shop that isn't used and if I took down the partition wall, it would make a nice extra section within the shop—' At this, he stopped and looked from his mother to Maisie. When no one spoke he continued. 'It would make a nice little section for you to sell some of your cakes and pies. It could work nicely for all of us, bring more people into the shop so they'd buy more vegetables from us and make a nice little profit for the two of you. What do you think?'

Maisie looked at Joyce who was deep in thought. 'But what about here? If Maisie is in town all of the time, I'll be right back to square one, with no help.'

'No, you are a lump, Jed Campbell,' Pru cut in. 'What he should have said was, maybe on market day and when any festivals are on. The town gets so busy then that I'm sure that would be enough. Every day would be far too much and I don't think poor Maisie would be able to bake that many pies for every day.'

'Oh, that's different. What do you think, Maisie? Would you like to do that?' Mrs Campbell put down her sewing and looked at Maisie.

'I should like to give it a go. You were only saying the other day that you could do with some new curtains for the sitting room and the carriage could do with some repairs.' Maisie thought for a moment. 'But it really is up to you, Joyce. Would you be happy for me to give it a try?'

It was settled and the four sat around the table with steaming mugs of tea and a nice pie for Jed and started to work out the details of how things should be run. When they were all satisfied, Jed and Pru made their goodbyes, with Jed promising that he would start the renovation work the next day.

The Grand Opening

Maisie was busy doing her morning chores, humming to herself as she collected the chicken eggs. She was sure that the chickens hid them from her: she would find them in the most peculiar places; up on rafters in the old barn; under clumps of grass out in the meadow. She didn't mind searching for them, she loved the feeling of being free and just being allowed to walk unhindered out in the fresh air.

Due to the size of the plot, she and Joyce had developed a method of calling her so that Joyce didn't have to shout; she said this made her feel like a fishwife and was very unladylike, so instead of shouting she would clang an old school bell that she had found in one of the sheds out back.

Maisie had just bent to look for more eggs when the bell started to clang. Looking towards the house, she could see Joyce standing on the porch, waving at her. 'Oh, I hope nothing is wrong,' she thought to herself and picking up her skirt, she ran towards the woman. 'What is it? Are you all right?' she puffed as she reached the steps to the porch.

'Yes, yes, I'm fine but we need to get into town. Apparently Jed has something to show us. Quickly, get changed, you don't want to go looking like that.' Joyce looked at the mud spatter on the girl's dress from where she had run through some mucky water in her haste to get back to the house.

By the time Maisie had changed and brushed her hair, Joyce had brought the carriage around to the front door. As soon as Maisie got up into her seat the carriage moved off, the little pony trotting and swishing its tail, happy to be out of the paddock.

'Has something gone wrong with the renovations?' Maisie looked at the older woman and frowned. 'Oh dear, I hope that everything is all right. I've worked out what to bake for Saturday and with all the fresh eggs I will be able to do something very special.' She stopped and looked at her companion, who hadn't uttered a word since leaving the farm. 'Are you sure that you're all right?'

The older woman just nodded and kept her eyes on the narrow lane. As the little carriage came over the brow of the hill, the town could be seen with its main street and the alleyways and side streets branching off it. Maisie always thought that from this position it somehow seemed at peace with itself; it wasn't until you got nearer that you could both see and hear the hustle and bustle of everyday life.

'Right, we'll leave the carriage here,' Joyce suddenly announced, pulling the little vehicle into a stable yard. 'Hi, Jim. Can I leave him here for a while, no more than an hour, is that all right?' The big blacksmith just raised his hand and carried on hammering the hot metal he was working into a horseshoe. Joyce securely tied the pony to a ring on the wall and giving him his muzzle bag with hay in, she hurried Maisie out of the yard.

After they had walked for a while, Joyce turned to Maisie. 'Right then, put this on.' She handed the girl a piece of cloth. 'Tight around your eyes, no peeking.' With that she took her hand and started to lead her along the pathway, until they came to a sudden stop and the blindfold was whipped off. At that precise moment clapping started and she realised that they were standing outside Jed and Pru's shop.

'Welcome to the newest pie shop in town,' Joyce sang out. 'Well, what do you think?'

Maisie couldn't believe her eyes; Pru had painted a sign that stood on the pathway. It read, "Welcome to Violet's Pie Shop, the very best of Bodmin Vale fayre".

'We thought we would use your middle name as it has a fresh countrified sound to it. Are you happy with that?'

Maisie was about to say that she didn't have a middle name when the conversation of that first day at Pond Farm jumped into her head. 'Yes, it's lovely,' she stammered, trying hard to hold back happy tears.

'Come in, come in.' Pru took Maisie's hand and led her through the rows of vegetables to the back of the shop, where they had put shelves up and she had her own little counter and till. Everything had been painted white and in bold blue writing along the top of the back wall, Pru had again painted, "Welcome to Violet's Pie Shop".

Maisie was overwhelmed and tears started to well up in her eyes.

'Don't you like it?' Pru asked. 'We can change anything that you don't like.'

'But I love it.' Maisie choked back her tears. 'I really love it.' Rushing into Joyce's arms, she gave the woman a huge hug and then Pru and Jed. 'How can I ever thank you?'

'By selling lots of pies, that's how,' Jed laughed. 'Are you going to be ready for Saturday? There's a huge market in town and it will be very busy.'

'Now I have all of this,' Maisie looked around at her lovely space, 'I'll be more than ready.'

'How about we all go and celebrate in the pub? It'll be nice for Maisie not to have to cook.' Jed and Pru looked at each other as Joyce continued, 'My treat.' With that the four happy companions set off across the street to the Anchor pub.

Maisie had been cooking for the last two days, making various pies, some individual and some larger: rabbit, chicken and vegetable, along with individual cakes and large family size ones. She had also made apple pies.

Saturday arrived bright but cold. As the two women loaded the little cart, Maisie's stomach began to churn. 'What if it doesn't work? After all the hard work that Jed and Pru have put into it?' She wouldn't be able to bear it.

'Well, I haven't yet met anyone who doesn't like your pies, especially the rabbit ones. I think your only problem will be stopping Jed from eating them all.' At this, the two women laughed and got into the cart to start their journey into town.

Once Maisie was satisfied that the pies were all set out properly, Pru proudly took the sign out and placed it on the pathway. An hour went by and no one bought any of the pies, although a few people came into the greengrocers for their vegetables.

Joyce could see that Maisie was deflated and started to think of a plan to get the ball rolling. 'If I went somewhere and someone that I didn't know had baked, I might like to try before I bought anything.'

Maisie looked at her friend.

'When you go to the grocer and he has, oh, I don't know, let's say some new type of cheese, he has some cut up on the counter for customers to taste.' This was said without looking up from her sewing.

'Do you think that's what I should do? Cut up one of the small pies and ask Jed to put it on his counter?' As she spoke, she selected a nice rabbit pie. 'It wouldn't hurt, I could cut this one up,' she held up the rabbit pie, 'and perhaps this.' In her other hand she had one of her cakes.

'It's certainly worth a try. Go and ask Pru and tell her she's in charge of stopping Jed's hand from wandering onto the plate.' With a nod of her head the older woman fell silent.

'Hello, Mrs Down. How are you today?' Pru spoke in a cordial manner to a favourite customer. 'Whilst I get the potatoes for you, can I interest you in trying some of this?' She held up the two plates to the woman. 'Take my word for it, they are truly delicious.'

To Pru's delight, on finishing her purchases at the greengrocer's counter, Mrs Down walked over to the pie stall. 'I'll take one of those rabbit pies and that cake.' Maisie was delighted and when the customer had gone gave Joyce a huge hug. If she could, she would have done cartwheels through the shop, she was that excited at her first sale.

After that it was non-stop until well after lunchtime. Nearly all of Maisie's baking had sold and she was just about to pack the remaining pies away when a young lad came running into the shop.

'Please, miss, don't tell me I'm too late, my ma will kill me. She wants a rabbit pie and a chicken one. She sent me out ages ago but I got sidetracked watching the cattle auction. You have got some left, haven't you?'

Maisie bent over the basket and fished out the two that he had asked for. 'Here you are, but you're lucky. That's the last of those.' The relief on his face made Maisie laugh. As he handed over the money a thought struck her. 'Just a minute, do you like cake?'

'Do I like cake? My ma says I'll eat her out of house and home. I don't like cake, I love it, why?' came the cheeky reply.

'Well then, I'd better help your ma by giving you this.' She handed him one of the individual cakes. 'Now, if you like it you must promise to tell all of your friends about my wonderful cakes.'

Taking a huge bite, his eyes lit up. 'I most certainly will.' Crumbs sprayed from his mouth as he spoke. 'Thank you, miss.' And off he went with his pies safely stored in the box his mother had sent him with, scoffing back the cake as if there was no tomorrow.

Joyce stood up and stretched. 'Come on, dear, let's go home. We've both had a long day.'

Joshua

After the old woman had stormed out of the house Mrs Green went to find out from Joshua exactly what all the urgency had been about. Walking into his study, she found him still sitting in his chair with his head in his hands.

'Joshua, what on earth has happened? Is Violet all right?'

He lifted his head to look at her. She was taken aback that tears were streaming down the young vicar's face. Slowly, without a word, he walked over to the painting.

'She said that it was such a shame that someone with such a beautiful face had such a wicked soul.' As he spoke he stroked the face which he had lovingly painted. 'She said that Violet is a thief, taken her money and gone, run away.'

'Never. I don't believe it.' Elsie spoke as she slipped an arm around his shoulders. 'Now you come with me and we'll have a cup of tea and you can tell me exactly what that awful woman said.' She led Joshua out of the study and along the hallway to the kitchen. 'Ed, put that kettle on.'

Ed was about to say something but his wife gently shook her head so he busied himself making the tea.

Joshua sat at the big kitchen table, sipping the weak sweet tea that had been placed in front of him. 'What am I to do? I can't believe that is true.'

Elsie quickly filled her husband in with the few details that she had gleaned from Joshua.

'No way,' came the angry response from Ed. 'There is no way that the girl would do that. If you ask me there's some mischief afoot and don't you worry, dear.' With that he patted his wife's hand. 'We'll get to the bottom of it.' Looking directly at Joshua, he continued, 'Now, you need to pull yourself together. I don't mean to sound hard but the sooner we start digging, the better.'

Joshua took out a big white hanky from his trouser pocket and noisily blew his nose. 'You're right, Ed, but where to start?' A thought suddenly struck him. 'When Robert was here he mentioned something to me, I don't want to go into it all at the moment, but I think he may have some ideas on what to do. I'll contact him immediately. When he left here, he was going to Cornwall, so maybe he can call in on the way back.' He gulped down some tea. 'Yes, that's what I'll do.' This last comment was more to himself than anyone else.

Whilst Joshua busied himself contacting various dioceses in Cornwall and leaving urgent messages for Robert to contact him as soon as possible, Ed and Elsie stayed seated at the big kitchen table.

'I tell you, Elsie, something is amiss. That girl is no more a thief than I am, straight as a die, she is.'

Elsie looked at her husband's angry face. Joshua wasn't the only one who would miss the girl; they had both also grown very fond of her.

'Look, at lunchtime go down to the pub and see if anyone mentions anything. This afternoon a group of us have been invited to tea at Martha's. I think she wants to show off her new furniture, but you know how they all like to dish any juicy gossip. If there is any talk I'm bound to hear it there.' They both nodded.

'I'll let Joshua know what we plan to do.' With this she got up and walked out of the room.

After Ed had dropped Elsie at Martha's, he quickly made his way to the Blue Boy pub and as he pushed open the door, he was pleased to see that the place was nearly full. They say women can gossip but men are normally worse, he thought to himself as he found a seat at the bar and ordered a pie and a pint.

'Make the most of that pie, I doubt there'll be any more,' the man sitting to his right commented, taking a swig of his beer.

'What do you mean? Jack always has plenty of pies.'

On hearing his name, the landlord walked over to join them.

The man continued. 'Haven't you heard? The young girl from over there,' he pointed out of the window towards a shabby cottage, 'has run off, took Mrs Durrant's money and scarpered. That's right, init, Jack?'

'Well that's what that young grandson of hers said when I saw him this morning. Said his grandma is heartbroken, apparently she loved the bones of the girl.' With this he shrugged his shoulders. 'Seemed such a lovely young lass as well, suppose you just can't tell.' With that Jack walked away to serve a customer who was getting impatient at the other end of the bar.

''Tis a shame, she made lovely pies.' The man stretched as he stood up to leave. 'Such a beautiful face as well, who would have thought?'

Ed sat at the bar, looking into his pint. He still couldn't believe that it was true. He contemplated marching across to the old hag and demanding to know the truth but thought better of it, as that brute of a son was known to be handy with his fists and he quite liked his face the way it was. After another hour with no other gossip, he was just leaving as Burt walked in. Sitting back down, Ed gestured to the man to join him.

'Let me buy you a pint, Burt. You've been through quite a lot today; I expect you could do with one.' Ed tried to make his voice sound as cordial as possible.

'Too damn true, driving all that way at the crack of dawn, bloody ridiculous.' Sinking the pint that had been placed in front of him in one go, he wiped his mouth with the back of his hand, banging the beer mug on the counter. 'Another, Jack, as quick as you like.'

'How about a whisky chaser?' Ed offered. 'I find now that driving any distance makes my poor old bones ache. Even taking Elsie over to Primrose Hill to visit her sister is a chore.'

'Huh, you want to try driving down to bloody Cornwall at the crack of bloody dawn and then turning straight round to drive all the way back, just because Ma's got a bee in her bonnet.' With that, he took another long swig of his beer and sinking the whisky chaser, slapped Ed on the back and was gone.

Arriving back at the rectory, Ed and Elsie went straight to Joshua's study.

'Did you find anything out? What's the gossip?' Joshua was sitting at the desk, a tumbler of brandy in his hand. Elsie noticed that the painting had been moved across the room and could now be seen from anywhere in the room.

Ed started by telling them both what had been said in the pub and what Burt had said about driving all the way to Cornwall. He left out the expletives, feeling that this language wouldn't enhance the story. He also commented on how strange Burt was acting, kind of edgy every time anyone came into the pub, as though he was expecting someone.

Elsie then took over. Apparently the group of woman had all heard the same story, that Violet was a thief and a no-good tramp; things such as, "I told my husband to stay away, a girl like that would do anything for money", and, "I've always said the prettier they are the more dangerous they can be", and so it went on until Martha turned to Elsie. With all eyes on them she remarked, "But surely, Elsie, dear, you knew her better than any of us. After all, she did spend a lot of time with the vicar at the rectory. Now what was it she did there? Oh, yes, cooking and painting, wasn't it?". Her voice, dripping with sarcasm, belied the sweet smile on her lips.

Elsie didn't want to make a scene as she felt that she needed to keep the women on her side. They might hear something and if she got shirty they were unlikely to tell her. "Yes, dear, that's right and a lovely girl we found her to be. I don't think that there are many in town that haven't tried her delicious pies". Hesitating, she continued, "I know that your husband was a regular customer at the pie stall". At this, she returned Martha's sweet smile, whilst a few of the assembled ladies coughed to cover up their giggles.

Elsie had been glad when she'd seen Ed pull up outside and had quickly walked out to join her husband. As she went to climb up next to him, a voice from the doorway called to her, "Elsie, wait". Turning, she saw Dora hurrying to catch her up.

"I didn't want to say in front of that lot", she inclined her head towards the little cottage, "But I did see something funny in the early hours of this morning. I heard a clatter out in the back yard and got up to see what it was. Well, I could have sworn that when Burt pulled the wagon out of the yard, Violet was sitting next to him. Then this morning when I heard all the gossip, I told my John what I'd seen and he said I must have been dreaming, 'cause what reason would they have to make up such a story?". She stopped and looked from Elsie to Ed. "But I would swear on the bible that it was Violet". At that moment the door to the cottage opened and some of the other woman could be heard making their goodbyes. "Anyway, I thought I'd tell you". With that, Dora hurried off down the street.

Joshua had sat quietly listening intently to every detail being relayed to him. Looking down into his brandy glass, he finally spoke.

'What have those devils done with her?' The anger and bitterness in his voice was palpable. 'Right, I have left messages all over Cornwall for Robert, but now that we know about Burt's journey this morning it is even more urgent. Robert took one of my pencil sketches of Violet with him the other day.' Seeing the astonished look on the couple's faces, he covered up the real reason by continuing, 'He thought that the painting was beautiful and wanted to show it to friend of his.' At least that was true. 'But I wouldn't let him take it so he made do with one of my sketches.'

Leaving the two men together in the study, Elsie made her way to the kitchen to start getting some dinner ready. She guessed that Joshua had not eaten since breakfast.

As soon as the door had shut, Ed sat down at the desk opposite Joshua.

'This is indeed a rum old do. Why would Burt be taking Violet away? And if that's true, why say that she just ran off? It doesn't make any sense.'

Joshua bowed his head. 'I'm afraid that something dreadful has taken place. Like you, the thought had crossed my mind: why not tell the truth? If Violet had wanted to leave of her own free will, why all the cloak and dagger stuff?' Joshua thought about what Robert had told him with regard to Burt and Daniel being paid to kidnap Violet, or Maisie, as she had previously been known. Had someone else paid them to get rid of her? He shuddered at the very thought. Looking across the desk at Ed, he finally spoke. 'I think that there's something that you and Elsie need to know.'

After swearing them both to secrecy, Joshua relayed the story just as Robert had to him. When he had finished Elsie was in tears and Ed asked, 'Why did no one come looking for her? And why didn't she try to escape? She had plenty of opportunity to either tell you or us.' His hand moved between him and his wife.

'Robert told me that the rumour around the town, spread by her own grandmother, was that the girl was a tramp and no good.' He swallowed hard before continuing. 'And then when a young woman's body was found and declared to be Maisie, in a way her fate was sealed.'

'Poor little thing, I wish that she had told me,' Elsie choked through her tears.

'This time she will not go missing, I won't allow it.' Joshua hammered his fist on the desk. 'This time someone does care. She will be coming home.'

Surprises

The following Saturday in Bodmin Vale was a horrible wet affair. All morning only two customers had come into the greengrocer's shop and that was more to get out of the rain rather than buy anything. By two o'clock most of the market stalls had been packed away and the miserable stall holders could be heard grumbling about the English weather and lack of money taken that day.

Maisie wandered up through the shop to the door and stared up at the sky. 'I think that I might call it a day, no one in their right minds is coming for pies today.' Hugging her shawl around her shoulders, she walked back to her counter and started to pack everything up carefully. 'Not sure what I'm going to do with these, they won't last until next Saturday,' she shouted across to Pru. 'I'm just going out the back, won't be long.'

Pru was also thinking of shutting up for the day. 'No point staying open,' she muttered as she walked around the counter and crossed to the shop door. As she was just about to put the closed sign up, a fine-looking gentleman pushed the door open a crack.

'Are you shut?' he enquired.

'Oh, no, sir.' Pru stepped away from the door and the man entered, turning to shake water from his hat. 'What can I get you?'

'I've actually come to buy some pies.' He spoke very softly. 'I have it on very good authority that they are splendid.'

A door slammed shut towards the back of the shop.

'Maisie, you have a customer.' Turning to the man she said, 'She won't be long, can I get you a seat?'

As he was about to answer, Maisie walked through from the back with her arms filled with boxes.

'Can I help you with those?' the man gently asked.

Startled, Maisie's head snapped up. The boxes scattered everywhere. Standing stock still, she found herself looking into the eyes of Joshua.

'Oh, my dear, I'm sorry to have startled you. Please don't be afraid.' As he walked towards her she backed away.

Pru stood open-mouthed, watching this encounter, not sure if she should call for Jed, who as usual was dozing in the back room.

'Maisie, I have searched the whole of Cornwall for you and it was only through the misfortune of my horse losing a shoe that I happened upon this place.' He stopped and gazed at her. 'Please, don't send me away.'

Maisie couldn't take her eyes off his face. She had thought that she would never see him again.

'Oh Joshua, I don't want you to go!' With that, she rushed sobbing into his arms.

Pru couldn't move, she had never seen anything like it. Why had he searched the whole of Cornwall? Surely her friends knew where she was.

Turning to face Pru, Joshua said, 'Madam, I know that this must all seem very odd but everything will become clear, I promise you. Now, Maisie, where have you been living and with whom?'

'She lives with me, sir. What's your business here?' Joyce appeared from the back room where she had been half dozing whilst doing her sewing.

'It's okay, Joyce, this is the gentleman that I told you about from Puddle Bridge.' Maisie stood still, clutching Joshua's hand as if she was afraid that he might disappear. 'Can we go back to Pond Farm and talk about everything there? I feel that it might be better.'

Joyce had turned pink; she hadn't realised that she was talking to a vicar. How rude she must have seemed. 'Yes, yes, of course,' turning on her brightest smile. 'You must excuse my sharpness, sir, but it was only to protect the girl.'

'No apology needed,' he reassured her. 'Now, can I help load your cart? The rain appears to have stopped so now might be a good time to make a move.'

The two women rode in the cart, with Maisie constantly turning to ensure that Joshua was still following them.

'Maisie, dear, please stop. He's not going to disappear in a puff of smoke.' Joyce gave the girl's hand a reassuring pat.

Once at Pond Farm and with everything packed away, Joyce led Joshua into the best sitting room.

'Now then, I think I deserve an explanation of exactly what is going on.' Joyce, ignoring Maisie, directed her question to Joshua.

Maisie looked from Joshua to Joyce and in a very quiet voice she stated, 'It's better if I explain.' She explained about her mother death and being taken to her nana. With a heavy heart she told Joyce about her little sisters.

Joshua stroked her hand. 'Oh, my dear, I didn't know. Did your grandmother ever tell you who took them?'

Maisie shook her head and wiping a tear from her cheek, she continued with the story. When she reached the part which included Joshua, he took over and very eloquently gave Joyce the facts. The whole story from start to finish took several hours and at the end Joyce just sat looking at them, shell shocked.

'Well, if someone other than the two of you had told me such a tale I would have called them a liar, so fanciful it is.' Joyce sat in deep thought and then, 'We must do something about that sister of mine and good-for-nothing nephew, but what? They need to pay for what they have put you through and as for that grandma of yours, well I just don't have words for her!'

Joshua bent his head and raising it, he looked at Maisie. 'With regard to your grandmother,' he coughed, 'I'm afraid I have some bad news. No one knows really why or by whom, but she was found dead in her cottage a while back.'

Maisie's hand flew to her mouth. 'Murdered, you mean?' He just nodded.

'Huh. Well, I'm sorry, Joshua, and I hope that she didn't suffer too much, but from what you've told me, death was too good for her,' Joyce was very matter-of-fact, 'After what she did to her granddaughters.'

By the time they had finished talking it was eleven thirty.

'Now, I don't think that it would be safe for you to travel back to town tonight, the lanes are bad enough in the dark when you know them.' Joyce stood up. 'Come with me and I'll make you up a bed in the back room, is that all right?'

Joshua kissed Maisie's hand. 'See you in the morning.' He followed Joyce out of the room.

The next morning was cold but bright. Being a Sunday, the church bells were ringing and echoed around the vale. On entering the kitchen Maisie found Joshua and Joyce deep in conversation.

'Ah, there you are.' Joyce poured some tea into a china cup from the big earthenware teapot. 'Joshua and I were just talking about what to do now.' She stopped and took a bite of her toast. 'I have asked Jed and Pru to leave the boys with Pru's mum and come up as soon as they can. We need to decide on a plan of action.'

After they had finished breakfast, Maisie asked Joshua if he would like to take a walk. She needed to clear up a few things with him out of earshot of Joyce. The air was fresh and tingled on her skin as they walked down the steps and onto the grass. Once some distance from the house Maisie stopped and looking out over the town she asked, 'Do the townspeople really think that I'm a thief?' Without waiting for him to reply, she added, 'And my friends – Peggy, Cook, Jennie and Bessie, they really all think that I'm dead?' With that, her voice caught in her throat. 'Why did she do this to me? I worked hard for her, I don't understand why she hated me so.'

Joshua looked at the woman he loved and felt his heart was breaking at her sadness. 'No one will think badly of you once the truth is known and as for your friends, they will be over joyed that you are still alive.'

'But if it's not me in that grave, then who is it?' Anxiously she twisted her fingers together. 'Just another person who nobody wanted.'

The Trap

Jed and Pru had just arrived at Pond Farm as Maisie and Joshua came back from their walk. The kettle was already boiling and Joyce had laid the table for morning coffee. Jed was already eyeing up the different cakes, trying to decide which to go for first. Pru sat opposite him, laughing.

'Will you look at your son, he's almost drooling! Honestly, Joyce, anyone would think that I never fed him.' Joyce chuckled as Pru continued, 'The trouble is, the boys are getting as bad, they never seem to fill up.'

As the big brown teapot was placed on the table they all sat down.

'Well how much do you two know?' Joshua asked as he took his place next to Maisie. 'Has Joyce had a chance to fill you in?'

'Somewhat, but it all seems so fanciful, I really can't get me head around it.' Pru shrugged her shoulders as she spoke. 'You may have to go over some of the details, if you don't mind.'

He started to explain the situation in as simple terms as he could. Pru asked several questions, so he very patiently went over details again and again. They really needed to have all the facts or things wouldn't go smoothly, and they would only have one chance at trapping the Durrants. When he had finished he asked the two of them to confirm that they fully understood what had happened up until that day. They both nodded and confirmed the details.

As Joshua was now satisfied, he started to tell the others what he had been thinking. 'Joyce, I would guess that you know your sister better than anyone. Maisie has really only seen the mean side of that family, but surely there must be some good hidden away under all of the sourness.'

'Huh, don't you bank on it.' Frowning, Joyce continued. 'My sister is a devil. I'm sorry, Joshua, I know that you're a vicar and all, but she is and always has been pure evil. If you can find a good side you're a better man than most. Why do you think that Jed was so worried when Maisie arrived? Sure he was because the police must be on her trail.'

'I always like to believe that everyone has a little humility in them, but I am quickly coming to the opinion that I am wrong in this case.' Joshua's hand instinctively went to the cross hanging around his neck. 'But we have to figure out a way of getting her and Burt to both come here.'

They all sat in silence, each trying to think of a reasonable way to entice the pair to Bodmin Vale.

Jed reached across the table towards the plate of cakes.

'For goodness' sake, Jed, can you stop thinking about your belly and concentrate on a plan?' Pru snapped at her husband.

'But I think better on a full stomach,' came the sheepish reply.

Maisie pushed the plate towards him and winking at Pru, said, 'Well, we shall all look forward to the most wonderful plan then, Jed, because after this fourth cake your stomach must be well and truly fit to burst.' The rest of the group started to laugh as Jed took a huge bite of a jam tart.

Joshua, who had been sitting quietly for the last half an hour, suddenly sat upright. 'I've got it! I think I know how to get them here.'

The others instinctively leaned forward as he continued.

'Joyce, I need to pretend that Maisie has done something truly awful and that you do not want her here any more. But you must insist that she comes down here to discuss it and not just send Burt.'

'How am I to do that? I don't think that she will travel this far.' Joyce rested her arms on the table and shook her head. 'In fact, I'm sure that she won't.'

'She will if she thinks that you're going to involve the police if she doesn't come down. She won't want the police delving into how Maisie got here in the first place. But we have to think of something so bad that she'll be afraid not to come.'

For the next hour or so the group went over different events. Maybe she got into a fight, was one idea or perhaps she was found drunk in the gutter. This one came from Jed. On and on they went, but nothing really seemed right.

'Well, she's told everyone in Puddle Bridge that I'm a thief, so why not make her prediction come true?' Maisie suddenly blurted out. 'I could have stolen something from the church and the vicar has stated that if you cannot get someone else in the family to take me, he will press charges and the full weight of the law will come down on my head.' She stopped for breath before continuing. 'Joyce, you could tell her that I've threatened to tell everything if I'm arrested. If that doesn't get her here, nothing will.'

Everyone around the table agreed that it sounded like a brilliant plan, but it was up to Joyce to convince her sister to make the journey, and she needed to do it as soon as possible.

'But what I don't understand is, what are we going to do with them once they get here?' Pru looked very puzzled.

Joshua explained. 'Well, once the truth comes out they won't be welcome in Puddle Bridge, so I am going to suggest that they move right away, possibly go over to Ireland. I believe you have relatives still living there?' He looked at Joyce for confirmation. 'But the sting in the tail will be that she must sign over the cottage to Maisie. After all, I think that's the least she can do.'

Maisie had become very quiet.

'Do I really have to see them again?' Tears filled her eyes. 'I've been so happy here that I really don't want to go back to Puddle Bridge.'

'My dear, you don't have to. The cottage can be sold which will give you a nice little nest egg for your future. However, I will need to go back, at least for a short while.' Joshua took her hand. 'But I promise it won't be for long.' He had already started making plans in his head to ask his dear friend Robert Bird for the diocese, which would soon become vacant on the retirement of the present vicar.

And so the plot was set. Joyce contacted her sister and told her about the trouble that Maisie was causing and that she could not stay with her any more. At first the woman had refused to make the journey but on hearing that Maisie was going to "sing like a bird" to the police if she didn't come, she miserably agreed.

The day of their arrival, even the weather was miserable, with rolling mist coming in from over the moors that left a cold grey blanket covering everything. Maisie couldn't sit still, nervously pacing up and down the kitchen, stopping only to stare out of the window.

At precisely 11.00 o' clock Pru came racing into the kitchen. 'They're here, just pulled in from the lane,' she whispered.

Joshua jumped up. He gave Maisie a quick hug and sent her upstairs.

'Right, Joyce you know what to do.' With that, he walked through to the sitting room and closed the door.

As the old wagon came to a halt, Joyce walked out of the front door and stood, arms crossed, and glared at her sister and nephew.

'Fine lot you are, sending trouble to my door.' Without waiting for an answer she turned and walked into the hallway.

Mrs Durrant was the first to enter the house, moaning about how her bones ached and she'd give the good-for-nothing, what for when she got her hands on her. Burt entered a couple of seconds after his mother. 'I hope you've got the frying pan going and a good cup of tea. Bloody famished, I am.'

'I think that you have more important things to worry about than your empty stomach,' came the curt reply. Pointing to the sitting room door, Joyce continued, 'There's someone that wants to talk to you, and if you know what's best you'll keep a civil tongue in your head.' This was directed at her sister, and looking at her nephew she added, 'and you will keep your fists to yourself.'

'Oh, bloody hell, is it the bobbies?' the old woman was visibly shaken.

Without a word Joyce pointed to the door and the old woman and Burt gingerly entered the room.

'For Christ's sake what are you doing here,' the shock in the woman's voice was palpable as she laid eyes on Joshua, sitting in the chair directly in front of the door.

For the next couple of hours raised voices could be heard, mainly the old woman and Burt, and the low hum of Joshua's voice. Suddenly it all went quiet.

'Oh, my god, do you think they've killed him?' Pru clutched at Joyce's hand as the two women sat close to each other in the kitchen, waiting to hear the outcome of the meeting.

The door to the sitting room slowly opened and they both let out an audible gasp of relief as Joshua walked out of the room.

'You will be very pleased to know that Mrs Durrant has agreed to the terms presented to her.' He gave the ladies a little bow. 'Do you have a pen and paper, please, Joyce? I would like her to sign a full confession, which will be handed to the police should she or Burt ever show their faces in England again.'

Joyce hurried into the little study. On returning, she handed him the articles he had requested.

'Joshua, is it really over?'

He looked into the anxious face of the older woman. Smiling, he patted her shoulder and with that, turned to go back into the room. 'Oh, maybe you would like to break the news to Maisie. She must be fraught with worry.'

After another hour or so the door opened and Mrs Durrant and Burt stamped out. On seeing her sister, the old woman stopped. 'I suppose you are pleased with yourself, bullying an old woman and her poor defenceless son.'

Joyce couldn't help but burst out laughing. 'Bullying? If there was an award for bullying, dear sister, you'd win it hands down and "poor defenceless son"? Don't make me laugh, that brute has caused more injury to people than I care to know about.' Looking the two of them up and down, she said, 'I never thought I would say it but as far as I am concerned, you are no family of mine. Now get out of my house and don't ever let me see or hear from you again. You're a wicked old hag, now get out.' With that, Joyce stalked past the two of them and opened the front door. Standing to one side, she hissed, 'You heard me. Get out.'

Mrs Durrant pulled herself up to her full height and with her head held high, walked out of the door. Burt meekly followed and as he passed his aunt, he mumbled under his breath, 'I was looking forward to one of your big breakfasts.' On that note, Joyce slammed the door shut. With her back leaning on it she closed her eyes. 'Thank the dear lord.'

As she opened her eyes she realised that Maisie was standing at the bottom of the stairs at the other end of the hallway. She looked so pale, with her eyes as big as saucers. Joyce's heart went out to her.

'I don't know how to thank you all, I just don't.' Burying her face in her hands, Maisie for the first time in years shed tears of joy and not sadness.

Early the next morning Joshua left for the long journey back to Puddle Bridge. Maisie had begged him to stay but after assuring her that he would return as soon as possible, he had left. Maisie had walked at the side of his little carriage to the end of the muddy driveway and after one last hug, she stood at the edge of the lane, straining her eyes to watch him until he was completely out of sight. With a heavy heart she turned and walked back to the house.

Elsie and Ed were waiting anxiously for Joshua to return to the rectory and on hearing the crunch of the pebbles under the horse's hooves, Elsie had rushed to open the front door.

'Please tell me you have news, we have been so worried about you!'

'Ed, can you take the horse and wipe her down, please? She has worked hard for me today.' Putting an arm around Elsie's shoulders, he confirmed, 'Indeed, I have very good news but first, I need to wash the grime of the journey away. Perhaps you could get us all something to eat and I will tell you everything.' To Elsie's surprise, he gave her a little peck on the cheek and, whistling, made his way upstairs to his room.

After their meal and when Joshua had relayed most of the details to them about his search and the outcome, the three sat in his study, the two men with a glass of fine brandy and Elsie with a small glass of sherry.

'I still can't believe it.' Elsie sipped her drink. 'I knew they were a bad lot but never would I have believed the extent of their evil ways. Stealing would have been bad enough but kidnap, oh, my.' Every time she thought about the harrowing ordeal that Violet, who now she knew was really Maisie, had gone through, tears would fill her eyes. 'When will we see her, Joshua? We both miss her so much.'

Joshua explained that Maisie was reluctant to come back to Puddle Bridge and because of this, he had asked a huge favour of his friend Robert Bird, who in a few weeks' time would be ordained as Bishop of Cornwall, if he could be considered for the diocese that old Reverend Brown was vacating later that year.

After a while and looking at her husband, Elsie whispered, 'I don't want to sound selfish, but what will happen to us?' Elsie was now on the verge of tears, thinking that not only were they to lose Joshua, who had become like the son that they had never been blessed with, but also their home.

On hearing this, Joshua burst out laughing. 'But I just assumed that you would come with me. After all, I will still need a gardener and housekeeper and who else could I trust to help Maisie with the chores of a busy rectory?' At this last bit he blushed. 'As you would have guessed, I am hoping that she will agree to marry me, but as yet, have not dared to ask her.'

Elsie clapped her hands in excitement at this news and Ed raised his glass. The three companions sat until late into the night, discussing details of the move and the, hopefully, bright future that lay ahead for them all.

The Cottage

Joshua rose early and after enjoying breakfast with Ed and Elsie, he announced that he was going into the town to ensure that the Durrants had really left and to check on the state of the cottage. On hearing this, Elsie asked if she could go with him. 'I'd like to make sure that the gossips of the town know exactly what happened to Maisie.'

The night before, the three of them had agreed on a story that would be relayed to the townspeople. Looking at his wife, Ed gently reminded her not to go into too many details but to just stick to the broad facts and that if anyone tried to dig deeper, she was to say that she knew no more than what she had already told them.

Elsie frowned at him. 'What do you think I am, an idiot?' Picking up her bag and plonking her hat on her head, she clicked her tongue and walked out of the front door to join Joshua in the little carriage. Ed stood in the middle of the kitchen, a smile gradually spreading across his face. He knew how much his wife was going to enjoy putting the gossips right.

On the journey into the town, the two had decided that they would enter the cottage through the back door, as Joshua felt that he did not want to attract too much attention this morning. So after leaving the horse and carriage at the local stables, Joshua and Elsie crossed the road and walked down the cobbled alley to the cramped and smelly back yard. Elsie shuddered at the smell. 'You wouldn't let pigs live in this,' she grumbled as she delicately picked her way through the filth and debris towards the back door.

'I think it best if I go in alone at first, just to ensure that no one is still here.' Joshua tentatively stepped over the threshold and after calling several times with no reply, he beckoned Elsie to join him.

The cottage looked as though it had been ransacked. Cupboard doors were left open with contents spilling out and stale food was still on the big table in the centre of the room. Everywhere looked dirty and unloved. 'How do people live like this?' Elsie, who was holding a handkerchief to her mouth and nose, looked at Joshua. 'Poor Maisie.'

'I'd like to get the place tidied up a bit if that's possible.' He looked around as he spoke. 'I thought maybe Ed would give me a hand, I think we need to do some minor renovations. I thought that I might approach Mr Gladstone, he buys up a lot of these cottages for the men who work on his land to live in with their families.'

Elsie agreed that it would be a brilliant idea to approach the local landowner and was secretly glad that Joshua had not included her in the cleaning of the place; the cottage gave her the creeps.

Excusing herself, she made her way to Martha's house, where she was sure that a few of the local gossips would be holding court over morning coffee. After putting them in the picture and calling in to tell Dora that indeed she had not been dreaming, but had seen Violet, Maisie, in the wagon with Burt on that fateful morning, she walked back to the stables with a satisfied grin on her face. Just as she had thought, four of the biggest gossips were all there. How they had enjoyed the details of what had happened and she was happy in the thought that before nightfall the whole of the small town would know all about it.

Later that day, the tall dark man stood in the shadow of an alleyway. He had been there for a while, listening to the two women gossiping on a doorstep.

'Well, she should know,' said one. 'After all, she's the vicar's housekeeper and it was him who tracked her down.'

'And you say that this girl is really called Maisie and not Violet?' the other asked. The man's ears pricked up at this part of the conversation.

'That's right. Paid they were to bring her here, then they tell everyone she's a thief when it's them breaking the law,' the first woman continued. 'Never did trust those Durrants, horrible lot if you ask me and this has just shown how evil they really are.'

'Gone to Ireland, you say?' The second woman continued to try to get as much information as she could, this was too juicy to let go. 'What about the girl, where's she then? Has she gone to Ireland as well?'

'No, staying in Cornwall apparently. The Durrants' cottage is being sold. I think that Mr Gladstone might buy it, thought about your John and his missus, I expect. You're a bit cramped, all of you living together.' Without waiting for confirmation, 'Might be worth him asking when he goes in tomorrow, get in early I always say. Anyway, better get on, I want to call on Mary. She hasn't been well and she'll enjoy a bit of news.' With that the woman hurried off down the street, all the while hoping that no one else had beaten her to Mary's house.

Once the tall man was sure that the coast was clear, he stepped out of the shadows. 'Ireland? Well, I'll be blowed.' Pulling his hood down over his face, he made his way back up the hill to his camp site. Smiling to himself he thought, "well at least Maisie is safe."

The next few days were frantic, with Joshua and Ed working from early morning to late into the night at the cottage. Ed had mended and repaired all of the woodwork; cupboard doors now fitted and the broken-down cupboard in the little scullery room at the back of the house had been replaced with shelves. The old sink and flagstone floor had been scrubbed and now, even though not perfect, it looked a hundred times better.

Joshua had whitewashed all of the rooms; the fireplace had been blackleaded and everywhere now looked bright and clean. The small back yard had been a challenge for the men; they decided in the end to get Mr Tattersall, the rag and bone man, to come and take away whatever he wanted. To their delight he cleared the yard completely and had given them a few pennies for the scrap, which was spent on a pie and a pint in the pub at lunchtime. They then set about washing down and scrubbing the yard, which had the desired effect of getting rid of the dreadful smell.

Elsie came and gave the place the once-over, exclaiming, 'It is now fit to sell!' On that note of approval, Joshua went to see Mr Gladstone in his office.

'Well, I shall have to inspect it, but if it is as you say, Vicar, then I shall be only too pleased to take it off your hands.' Hesitating, he added, 'For the right price, of course!'

Everything seemed to be moving at such a quick pace that Elsie kept saying to anyone who would listen, 'My head is all of a spin.' This always made Joshua and Ed smile at each other as Elsie's head was always in a spin, crisis or not.

Mr Gladstone confirmed that he would purchase the cottage and the paperwork was drawn up by his solicitor. The only fly in the ointment was that Maisie, who was now the owner, needed to be present to sign it.

Joyce called Maisie into the kitchen and sitting her down, explained. 'Joshua has been in touch, dear.' Looking at Maisie's worried face, she quickly went on, 'You need to go back to Puddle Bridge. The cottage can't be sold unless you sign the paperwork in front of the solicitor. I can go with you, if you'd like me to? And Jed has said that he will happily drive us in his wagon, which will be a lot more comfortable than the little carriage.' She stopped and looked at the girls worried face. 'Maisie, it's all right. They've gone and Elsie has made sure that everyone knows that you are not a thief. I promise that you have nothing to be afraid of.'

Maisie looked at the kind face of her friend. 'One thing puzzles me. How did the Durrants ever manage to buy a cottage? Most people struggle to pay rent and would never in a lifetime be able to buy somewhere.'

'My sister's husband, Franklin Durrant, was a kind and generous man, very well-to-do, with quite a bit, or so I believe. Family money. When my sister was young she was a very nice-looking girl.' Maisie looked shocked; the woman she had known was a grizzled-up, wrinkled old biddy.

'Franklin thought the world of her and when Burt was born, he was over the moon. He owned a small mill firm on the edge of town, employed quite a lot of the men from the town who all liked him. He was a very good boss.' She stopped, looking down at her hands. 'One day a dreadful accident happened. A fire was started by one of the big grinding machines, which had got overheated. Franklin made sure that all of the men were safe but unfortunately, in doing so he was trapped at the back of the building and couldn't escape. My sister had hurried to the mill and on hearing that Franklin was still inside, had tried to rush through the flames to get to him.' She stopped, her voice cracking with emotion. 'That's how she got all the dreadful scars on her face and hands. Franklin had left her a young and wealthy widow, but nothing or no one could ever replace him and after his funeral she took to the drink and the decline started.'

Maisie stared at her companion. 'Oh, my goodness. How awful. I can't imagine how that must have felt.'

'But my dear, even though she had such a terrible experience it still doesn't excuse the wicked things that she has done. Those were done from her own choosing and cannot under any circumstances be excused.' Patting the girls hand, she said, 'Now we must be ready early tomorrow morning. Joshua will meet us at the solicitors and then everything in Puddle Bridge will be ended.'

The light was fading as they approached Puddle Bridge. Making their way through the town, Maisie was pleased that most people would already be at home, with the curtains closed. Mr Johnson, the solicitor, was a kindly man and had agreed to meet Maisie at the rectory to save her having to run the gauntlet of the old town gossips and the curtain-twitchers. He was already enjoying a glass of brandy with Joshua in the study, when the wagon pulled into the driveway.

On seeing Maisie, Elsie rushed forward. 'Oh my dear, it's so good to see you!' Both women hugged each other and cried. 'I can't believe that you are really here,' the older woman said as she stroked Maisie's hair. Looking over her shoulder, Maisie caught sight of Ed, who was hovering near the doorway, moving from one foot to the other. He had also wanted to rush forward on seeing the girl but thought it best to stay back and let his wife greet the trio first. To his delight, on gently releasing herself from Joyce's arm's, she ran over to him and flinging her arms around his neck, gave him a biggest hug he had had in a long time.

'It's lovely to see you both!' Then, remembering her manners, she beckoned Joyce and Jed over and introduced them.

'Maisie, Joshua has asked that you join him and Mr Johnson in the study. Why don't the two of you come with me?' Looking at Jed, she continued, 'I'm sure a nice cup of tea and something to eat would be welcome. Ed, can you take the wagon around the back and then join us in the kitchen?'

Mr Johnson went over the paperwork with Maisie and was visibly shocked at how educated she was. After listening intently to the man and asking just a couple of questions, she sat down at the big desk. Hesitating with the pen in her hand, she looked at Joshua, who nodded and with that, she signed her name to the document.

'The money will be available tomorrow afternoon. I suggest that maybe Joshua and that fine figure of a man that you arrived with come to collect it. It is a lot of money and I would not suggest that a young lady should walk around the streets alone with it.'

After Mr Johnson had gone, Maisie slowly stood and walked over to the painting that was now hanging in pride of place on the study wall.

'Oh, Joshua, it is beautiful. Is that how you really see me?'

Standing next to her, he carefully said, 'Trust me, my dear, the painting does not do full justice to your true beauty.' Looking down into her eyes, he added, 'A painting can only show the world the outside beauty of a person and cannot capture the inner strength of the person's soul.' With that, for the first time, he tenderly kissed her.

Maisie's Wish

As it was so late in the evening when Mr Johnson left the rectory, Joyce and Jed stayed over, Elsie bustled around organising bedding and after they had all eaten, she showed them to their rooms. They had agreed to stay over the following night as well, to allow Jed to go the solicitor's office with Joshua. Mid-afternoon the next day, the two set off to collect Maisie's money.

After their departure and leaving Joyce and Elsie sitting in the kitchen, regaling each other with tales about their lives, Maisie had wandered out into the garden. Although the sun was out, the wind had a cold, bone-chilling feeling to it.

'It's coming from the north,' Maisie heard Ed say. 'That's why it's so cold. Come on in here and warm up.' She realised that he must be in his little shed at the end of the garden. Walking over, she found him sitting on an upturned wooden case. He gestured to another that he had already put an old sheet over. 'Sit yourself there and tell me what you're worrying about.'

Ed had always been able to tell when she was worrying or confused about something. Sitting down, she hugged her coat around her slender figure.

'I know that this should be one of the happiest days of my life and by the end of it I shall be richer than I could ever imagine.' She stopped and looked at the kindly old man. 'But I can't help but wish that my dear friends at the Park knew the truth.' She shuffled her feet on the shed floor. 'I hate the thought that they all think that I am dead, especially Peggy. I often think of her. She must have gone through so much when she found that I was missing and I know that she would never have forgiven herself for leaving me alone.'

She sounded so sad that Ed had to swallow hard before he could answer her. 'What are you saying, Maisie? What do you want to do?' although he thought that he already understood, he needed her to tell him.

'I want to see them all again, so that I can explain that I am not bad and that I didn't run away and that I am certainly not dead. I would like to hug Peggy and tell her that what happened was not her fault. Even if she had stayed with me for the entire day, they would have found a way of kidnapping me.' She looked up at the old shed roof where a spider was spinning a very elaborate web. 'Cook was so kind to me throughout my time there, as was Jack, Miss Brockenhurst and Lady Elizabeth. I hate the thought of them thinking that I just upped and ran away without a word.'

At that moment, Joyce called from the kitchen for them to come in as Joshua and Jed were back. As they stood, Ed hugged the girl. 'Leave it to me, love, let me see what I can do. Now come on, your ladyship, your money's waiting.' He teased her with a very elaborate bow and straightening up, offered her his arm. Linked together they walked back up the garden path and into the warmth of the kitchen.

The next morning Jed and Joyce said their goodbyes to Elsie and Ed. Joyce hugged Elsie and told her how much she was looking forward to having such a lovely lady as a friend when they moved to Cornwall. Turning to Maisie, she said,

'Look after yourself. Don't worry about the pie stall, it will still be there when you come back. Until then Pru and I will muddle through.'

Jed shook Ed's hand and the two exchanged pleasantries about helping each other after the move. With one hand, he helped his mother up into the wagon whilst in the other, he had a wonderful pie, "For the journey". The little group stood at the rectory door and waved until the wagon was out of sight. Turning, they filed silently back into the house.

'Maisie, can I talk to you for a moment?' Joshua opened the study door and ushered her in. 'Ed has told me that you would like to go back to the Park, is this right?'

Maisie had seated herself next to the fire and without taking her eyes off the flames, she said, 'I really would, Joshua, just to let them know the truth. I hate the thought of Peggy going through the rest of her life thinking that she was the cause of my death.'

'Why didn't you tell me?' He knelt at her feet. 'Maisie, dear, I would try to grant you any wish you wanted. If this will ease your mind then we shall do it.' He stood. 'But first I will check with Reverend Douglas – I'm assuming that he is still presiding over the church on the estate – that your friends are still there. My dear, you will need to be patient. It could take him a day or two to come back to me.'

'Thank you,' was all she could manage to say and so the wait began.

It was almost a week before Joshua heard back from Reverend Douglas. He explained that he had been away at a conference, but yes, indeed the individuals that he was asking after still resided at the Park. Joshua asked him not to mention the enquiry to anyone, as a surprise was being put together. The older vicar agreed and so the plan started to take shape.

On a crisp, bright morning Elsie knocked on Maisie's bedroom door. Entering, she opened the curtains and sitting herself in the chair next to the bed, looked at the young girl, who was stretching and rubbing her eyes. 'Have I overslept? What time is it?'

Elsie gave a little laugh. 'Today, my dear, your wish will come true. Oh, listen to me! I sound like a fairy godmother; all I need is a wand.' She gave another little chuckle. 'Get yourself up and washed. Oh, and if I were you I would put on your very best outfit, you know, that lovely blue one.'

'What is going on?' But even as she asked the question, Elsie had already shut the door and could be heard going down the stairs.

She did what she was told and carrying her coat over her arm, she descended the stairs. Some sort of commotion was happening in the kitchen and as she entered, she found Elsie packing a picnic basket with various goodies.

'Surely it's too cold for a picnic?' Maisie looked from Elsie to Ed and then at Joshua. 'What is going on? First, I'm told to put on my best outfit and now a picnic basket. What nonsense is this?' She firmly sat down at the table 'I refuse to move until someone,' looking straight at Joshua, 'tells me what is going on.'

Laughing, Joshua nudged Ed. 'Well, in that case, which do you want to carry, the picnic basket or this one?' he said, pointing to Maisie. 'Now, come on, don't be silly. I'm taking you out for a surprise. Don't spoil it.'

'Okay, okay, but I'm not sitting on damp grass in my best dress.' She was surprised when all three of them burst out laughing. 'Well, come on then. I'm ready and waiting.' She walked out of the kitchen and stood near the front door. Joshua was still chuckling as he flicked the reins and the horse started to trot forward. Looking back at the couple standing at the door, he waved happily and with that, they were on their way.

After about an hour and a half Maisie started to think that she recognised certain beauty spots and places along the way. Turning to Joshua, she suddenly blurted out, 'Are you taking me back to the Park?'

Joshua pulled on the reins until the carriage came to a complete stop. Looking at her frightened face, he gently said, 'I thought that you wanted to go back to let your friends know that you are safe and well. We can turn around, no one knows that you are coming.'

'Are you going to leave me there?' She felt herself tremble.

'Oh, Maisie, no. Of course not. I love you.' Suddenly he realised that he had finally said it out loud. Looking at her, he blushed. 'I never meant for you to find out this way, but I love you, Maisie, with all of my heart and if you will have me, I would like to be your husband.'

After what seemed like an age, with tears in her eyes she answered, 'I would like that.'

For only the second time, he held her face in his hands and placed the most gentle of kisses on her lips.

Holding her hands in his, he whispered, 'Good. Now that we have that out in the open, are you ready to meet your friends?' He flicked the reins again and the carriage jolted forward. After another couple of miles, he pulled the horse to the right and there in front of them, at the end of the long driveway, was the magnificent Wilton Park.

As they approached the lawn where that terrible incident had happened in the copse all those months ago, a man hurried around from the side of the house. Maisie recognised him as Reverend Douglas. Without acknowledging the girl he quickly walked around the carriage and whispered something to Joshua, who immediately turned the carriage towards the church.

It wasn't far and on reaching the arch which led to the graveyard, he turned to Maisie.

'Walk to the end of the path and turn to the right. Please don't ask any questions, just do this for me.' His eyes pleaded with her and without further question, she did as she was asked.

Her heart was beating so hard that she felt it might escape from her chest as she slowly and gingerly walked along the pebble path. The pebbles made such a noise that after a while, she stepped onto the grass and walked on in silence. Once or twice she glanced back to make sure that Joshua was still there.

Following the path round to the right, she suddenly stopped. A woman not much older than herself was kneeling next to a grave and for a moment Maisie felt awkward, not knowing what to do. She didn't want to be found gawping at the woman; neither did she want to intrude, so engrossed was the woman in tending the little grave.

She had just decided to turn back when the woman suddenly shouted, 'Maisie, get here, girl. What are you doing?'

Maisie opened her mouth to answer but as she did so, a little girl of about two appeared from behind a gravestone. Running over to her mother, she stopped and gave the sweetest smile.

'What are you smiling at, young lady?' came the terse response from the woman, who was still on her knees.

'That lady.' The little girl pointed at Maisie.

The woman visibly paled as she turned to look to where her daughter was pointing.

Maisie's hand went to her mouth as the other woman let out a loud scream.

'Peggy! Oh, Peggy, is it really you?' She walked towards the now-standing woman who was clutching the little girl to her. 'Please, Peggy, don't be afraid.'

'Are you a ghost?' The woman was visibly shaking as she spoke. 'Oh, dear God, our father.'

'Please, Peggy, I'm not a ghost.' Maisie kept slowly walking towards the other woman. 'I've so longed for this day.'

Opening her arms, Peggy suddenly leaned forward, pulling Maisie to her. As she did so, she hugged her so hard that she thought she might break.

The little girl looked from one to the other and then decided that grown-up stuff was boring and went off to explore again. The two women stood looking down at the little grave.

'But if this is not you, then who is it? Oh, Maisie, how could you have just gone off and left me?'

The two women talked for a while, next to the grave, and then walked over to a nearby bench that was under a big oak tree. Once seated, Maisie started to explain, as best she could, what had happened on and after that dreadful day. Peggy sat in stunned silence, not quite able to understand how these things could have happened.

Looking in the direction of the little girl, Maisie asked feeling confused, 'Maisie?' She looked at her friend.

'When the baby turned out to be a girl, no other name would do. At the time Brian and I thought it was a nice tribute to your memory.'

Maisie smiled. At least something nice had come from the day at the fair.

Peggy continued touching Maisie's hand. 'I still can't quite believe it. Promise you're not going to disappear in a puff of smoke in a minute, are you?

'I know Cook will be happy to see you, although I think that I had better break it to her gently, don't want her fainting or something.'

The two women, with the little girl skipping after them, walked back through the graveyard to where Joshua was waiting. On seeing them he jumped down from the carriage and after being introduced to Peggy, he turned to Maisie.

'Reverend Douglas has invited me to spend some time with him whilst you speak with your friends. Get someone to let me know when you're ready to leave. But not too late, we need to get back before dark.' With that he strolled away and disappeared through a nearby door.

'Cook, can you sit down for a minute, please? I have a surprise for you,' Peggy announced as she walked into the kitchen.

Cook looked at Jennie and winked. 'Oh, please don't tell me you're having another bairn.'

Peggy sniffed. 'If you want the surprise, you need to sit. If not – oh, well.' Shrugging her shoulders, she turned as if to leave.

'Oh, for goodness' sake, all right.' Cook shuffled over to the little table that still sat in the corner of the kitchen. 'Let's have it, then.' Sitting down, she placed her hands on her knees and sighed.

'Okay, you can come in.'

With that, the door was slowly pushed open and there stood Maisie.

'Oh, dear God, what is going on?' Cook stammered.

Bessie, who was also in the kitchen, and Jennie both stood, open-mouthed, looking towards the door.

Bessie finally managed to speak. 'Is it really you? I don't understand.'

After everyone had got over the shock of seeing Maisie, she told them what had happened and where she had been since that awful day.

'Wait here. I know that Lady Willaby will want to be told, I'll get Mrs Dean.' Cook could be heard talking to the other woman, who appeared, ashen-faced, in the kitchen. Again, Maisie had to describe what had happened and was quite glad to know that the family weren't at home that afternoon. She was now beginning to feel tired from telling the story so many times.

After a while she asked if someone could let Joshua know that she was ready to leave. She was both happy and sad as she climbed into the carriage next to him, as the day had turned out to be quite an ordeal. Promising that she would come back soon, she bid them goodbye and the long journey home began.

The Perfect Day

On waking, Maisie lay in her bed at Pond Farm and thought about the day ahead. Over the last few weeks so many things had happened that she still felt a bit dizzy when thinking of them all.

First came the ordination of Robert Bird as Bishop of Cornwall. What a day that had been! Maisie had attended with Joshua on their first formal public appearance as an engaged couple.

A week before the ceremony, Joshua had taken her to a beautiful cove for a picnic, with Joyce in attendance as chaperone. Whilst the older woman had dozed over her sewing, Joshua had got down on one knee and officially asked Maisie to be his wife. He had produced the most beautiful ring, an oval emerald with little diamonds surrounding it, explaining that the ring had been his grandmother's and then passed down to his mother. As both ladies were no longer with him, he wanted the next special lady in his life to have the ring. Maisie was delighted and squealed so loudly when he placed the ring on her finger that Joyce was startled out of her sleep. On hearing the news, she began to cry, hugging them both and shouting her congratulations into the wind.

Once they arrived back in Bodmin Vale, after the picnic, Maisie couldn't wait to show Pru. Walking into the greengrocer's she was for once glad to see the place empty.

'Oh, Pru, something dreadful has happened!' Trying hard to keep the excitement out of her voice she continued, 'You will never guess what Joshua has done.'

Her friend, fearing the worst, rushed around the shop counter and steering her to a chair asked, 'Oh Maisie, you look so strange. What on earth has happened?' Her concerned face made Maisie feel a little bit guilty. Unable to stall her any further, she suddenly started to laugh and cry at the same time.

'Maisie, for goodness' sake, what is it?'

'He's only asked me to marry him.' With that, she held out her left hand. 'I'm sorry to have tricked you but I'm so happy, I think that I may burst.' Jumping up, she hugged her friend, who was now also laughing and crying.

On hearing the commotion in the shop, Jed poked his head out from the back room and seeing the two women both crying, laughing and hugging each other, quickly withdrew into the room, muttering, 'I'll never understand women.'

On the day of the ordination, Maisie had chosen a lovely moss green dress as she felt that this would showcase her ring perfectly and as it was a lovely warm day, she matched this with a silk shawl and a little hat with a green feather in it.

On arriving at Pond Farm, Joshua's eyes shone with pride as Maisie walked out of the house to greet him on the porch. 'You look beautiful, my dear. I think a few of the other ladies may be a little jealous.'

Maisie blushed, she still couldn't get used to receiving compliments, but was happy in the fact that Joshua approved of her outfit. Joyce had helped her to embroider flowers and butterflies, very delicately placed around the hem of her dress and they had sat up late into the night to get it finished, so to hear the appreciation in his voice made it all worthwhile.

On reaching the town, the place was full of people who had all turned out to see the procession of the new Bishop. On seeing the hordes of people, they had decided to leave the horse and carriage in the blacksmith's yard, as Joshua felt that the crowds of people may frighten the horse and it would be easier to walk through the town and up the little hill to the cathedral. Checking that Maisie agreed that this was for the best, he pulled the carriage into the yard. Jumping down, he walked over to the big blacksmith to confirm that this would be okay and then returned to help Maisie down from the carriage.

As they walked through the town, several people stopped to congratulate them and ask when the wedding was going to be.

'Remember, I do lovely flowers,' one woman said.

'I make lovely wedding cakes,' another offered.

Joshua squeezed Maisie's hand and whispered, 'I do believe that they are as excited about a forthcoming wedding as we are ourselves.' Maisie doubted that anyone could even come close to the excitement bubbling up in her at the thought of being Joshua's wife, but just smiled at him and nodded.

As they entered the coolness of the cathedral, Joshua felt the eyes of the other vicars on them as they walked down the main aisle and took their places in the very front pews. Robert had insisted that his dear friend and his fiancée should be right at the front, much to the indignation of some of the older vicars. Joshua was so happy that he really didn't care what anyone else thought or said, as long as he had the woman he loved next to him.

After the pomp and ceremony of the ordination, the chosen few were taken by carriage to the new bishop's castle. This was set in a very romantic position at the top of a hill, overlooking the sea. Joshua was busy socialising and Maisie, feeling a little out of her depth, moved to one of the window seats and looking out over the rolling surf thought back over her life. She was daydreaming and didn't realise that someone was talking to her.

'Thinking of your wedding plans or just daydreaming?'

Turning, she saw a woman of about her own age standing there.

'I thought you might like this.' She handed Maisie a cup of tea. 'Do you mind if I join you? Only I don't know anyone here and feel a little lost.'

'Oh, I'm sorry. Where are my manners?' Maisie gestured to the woman to sit down. 'I'm Maisie,' she said, offering a hand to the woman.

'I'm Geraldine.' The woman blushed. 'I'm Robert's girlfriend, although at the moment it's a secret.' Looking down at her cup, she added, 'Although now that he's ordained, we are going to announce our engagement. Robert asked my father last week and thank goodness, he said yes. I think he quite likes the idea of having a Bishop in the family.' At this she giggled.

The two women sat and talked for the rest of the afternoon about everything and nothing and when Joshua came to tell Maisie that it was time to go, the two had become good friends and promised to meet again soon. Once safely in the carriage, Maisie asked Joshua if he had known about Geraldine, but he said he had not and found it strange that Robert hadn't told him.

'I shall have to tackle our new Bishop about that' he laughed. 'However, I have some news. The vicar at Clyst is retiring and Robert has asked me to take over the diocese.'

'But where is Clyst? I thought we were going to stay in Bodmin Vale?' Maisie was suddenly afraid. She didn't want to move again and leave all of her friends behind.

Smiling, Joshua took her hand. 'It's okay, both dioceses are now going to be available. Bodmin Vale is already without a vicar and when the old reverend retires in Clyst, the two dioceses will become one. We shall move into the rectory at Bodmin Vale and I will run them both from there. It also means that Ed and Elsie can move into the old church warden's cottage, which is in the grounds of the vicarage.'

Maisie smiled with relief. She had hoped that that would be the plan.

Lying in her bed, there was a knock on the door and there stood Joyce with a breakfast tray. 'I thought, as this is to be your last day at Pond Farm, that you should have breakfast in bed.'

'Oh, Joyce, thank you, you always think of the kindest things. But won't you join me?' Maisie wriggled up to a sitting position as Joyce placed the tray on her lap and sat down on the chair next to her bed.

She gave a little cough and shuffling her feet, she asked, 'Maisie, I don't know how much you know about being married and what to expect on your first night as a married woman, but if there is anything that you would like to know, please ask.'

Maisie looked at the older woman who had been kindness itself to her since her arrival at Pond Farm.

'It's okay, Joyce. Pru has already explained things to me. It all seems very strange but Pru said there's nothing to be afraid of.'

'Oh, good. As long as you know.' There was an audible note of relief in Joyce's voice. Changing the subject quickly, she continued, 'Your dress is so beautiful, we made a good job of that,' looking across the room to where Maisie's wedding dress was hanging on the outside of the wardrobe, 'and the weather looks set to stay fair as well.'

Pru arrived at the house at 10.00 am and after Maisie had bathed, helped her with her hair. She had decided that she would like to have a long plait with flowers entwined in it. Pru struggled with Maisie's thick curls but eventually the plait was done and the little white and yellow flowers looked lovely against the darkness of her hair. Slipping into her dress she suddenly shuddered and speaking mostly to herself, said quietly, 'My ma would have loved today.' Turning to look in the long mirror, she caught Pru's eye. 'Every girl should have her mother with her on her wedding day and her father to walk her down the aisle.'

Pru nodded. 'But Ed looks on you as a daughter and to be honest, a great father he makes as well. This will be one of his proudest moments. You do know that, don't you? He's been telling everyone who will listen how proud he was when you asked him to do the honours.'

'Maisie, your carriage awaits,' Joyce shouted from the bottom of the stairs. Maisie started to descend and on seeing Ed, smiled at him; he really did look so proud. Outside, Jed waited, suited and booted.

'How handsome you look, Jed,' Maisie said, making the man blush as he took her hand and helped her into the carriage.

People stood and watched as the bridal party made their way through the town, shouting congratulations and good luck messages as the carriage passed. On reaching the gate to the little church in the centre of the town, a group of women had gathered to catch a glimpse of the bride. "Oh, my, how beautiful", and, "gorgeous dress", and, "oh, she looks so young", were just some of the comments that could be heard.

Stopping at the church door, Maisie looked at Ed and nodded that she was ready. He gave her a peck on the cheek and they proceeded into the church.

The church bells rang out to announce the happy occasion as the now Reverend and Mrs Jones stepped out into the sunshine. Maisie looked around at the assembled guests and was so happy to see Peggy and Brian with little Maisie. Cook and Jennie had also been given time off to attend.

'Oh, look,' shouted little Maisie and everyone turned to look towards the church gate where, dismounting his bicycle, was the traditional chimney sweep.

No-one at the wedding would have guessed what had happened an hour before. The chimney sweep had been happily cycling to the wedding in anticipation of receiving a silver half-crown, when suddenly standing in front of him was a man dressed completely in black. He had knocked the sweep from his bike and pulling him into the wooded area surrounding the town, had instructed him to give him his waistcoat, trousers and cap. After handing these over, he had been gagged and tied to a tree.

'Now, don't struggle. I'll be back within the hour and you'll get your payment. But any noise—' with that, the deep growl of the man's voice trailed off. The chimney sweep sat in silence, nearly afraid to breathe.

With long strides, the sweep walked towards the assembled group. His face was black and his cap was pulled tightly down over his head. He was black from head to toe.

Ignoring everyone else, he walked straight to the bride and taking Maisie's hand in his, he gently placed a tiny gold locket in her palm.

Maisie gasped as she recognised the locket as the one that her ma had always worn. How had this man come into possession of her mother's locket?

Slowly and hesitantly, she brought her head up and looked straight into the eyes of her father.